STEALING FROM SELKIES

A SAPPHIC PARANORMAL ROMANCE

THE CRYPTIDS OF AMERICA
BOOK 6

KATRYNA LALOCK

1

ADDISON

There's nothing quite like the rush of getting fucked in a bathroom.

I prefer to do it in the men's restroom – it's dirtier, but there's also no line. There's less time to go back on the decision we've both made, to awkwardly laugh as we wait our turn. This bar is seedy enough not to care what we do, so long as it's hidden behind a stall door. I'd prefer out in the open, but that's a little rude. Some people just want to piss in peace and not watch someone getting slammed against the sink. Plus, it keeps people from washing their hands – which is a disgusting thought.

I can't help this train of thought. I have one of *those* minds, the ones that wander from thought to thought too fast for most people to keep up. Sometimes I'm on thought five or six before someone says, "Addison...

what does having sex in a bathroom have to do with washing your hands?"

Oh boy, let me tell you.

But back to the present because that's what my therapist says to do. When I find myself unable to connect or when I feel my brain spinning out of control, she always says to be aware of my five senses. What do I see? Smell? Hear? Feel?

Right now, I see the back of the toilet, where my fingers are splayed. I feel the guy ramming into me from behind, my skirt pushed up around my waist. The air in the bathroom is thick with humidity, likely due to its proximity to the beach. *Nope, you're drifting.*

He's gonna have to fuck me harder to keep my mind with my body.

I push back into him, driving the pace and fervor up. I want to feel his bare thighs against my backside, I want to feel the way our sweaty skin kisses and then sticks. I like the sound of our wet skin slapping, filling the small area with it.

Any minute, someone could angrily bang on the door and confront us. The louder we are, the more likely this is to happen.

Do I want to get caught? Maybe. Not really, I guess, because it would cut this whole thing short.

...but what if we did?

I'm drifting again.

"God, you feel good," mumbles the guy behind me.

Alec, that's his name. He's a handsome tourist who wandered into the bar by accident. He's from...oh, god, I don't remember. It's not relevant.

Alec feels good, too. It'd be better if I could concentrate. Never fear, I have an idea.

My purse is still slung across my body, mostly because I know better than to let it touch the ground in this shithole. I release my grip on the back of the toilet to dig through it and find my little pocket travel vibrator, perfect for such occasions. I flip it on and press it against my aching clit, moaning at the sensation.

"Is that a vibrator?" Alec asks, slowing his thrusts. This won't do, I've mustered just enough anxiety at the thought of getting caught to get me going again. His attempt to talk to me really pulls me out of my moment.

"Yeah, I'm getting an orgasm out of this one way or another," I tell him, shoving my ass back against him. If he was offended by the statement, or if it upset him, he's a good enough sport not to say anything. There are no reflective surfaces for me to see his face, which is a bit of a blessing. Dudes about to cum always look constipated to me.

Alec resumes his strokes, but he starts to lag a little. This won't do because the previous pace I set was much more to my liking. I need it fast, hard, deep – I need every single sensory button hit at the same time. I need the feel of his balls as he bottoms out, the way his fingers dig into my hips, the way my breasts bounce in my tight dress without a bra on. The fabric against my nipples is just enough friction, paired with the skin on skin.

Scent leaves something to be desired, but I can block that out for now.

The vibrator against my clit drums along level one, but I need more. I bump it up to level three, feeling as much as hearing the vibration as it presses against my sensitive bud. My insides clench against his dick, wanting to inhale every inch of it.

"Oh god," he murmurs. I know that sound. It's the sound of a dude about to cum. If I want to beat him to it or join him in it, I've got to up the ante.

"Is someone fucking in here?" comes a male voice outside the stall.

There it is, the exact push I need. All at once my orgasm hits me – I clench down on his dick, riding the waves as it rips through me. I press the vibrator harder against my clit, letting the sensation uncoil as it pushes through my stomach, spiraling out into my chest.

Alec is close, too. He drives his dick in to the hilt, his hips now making slow, jerking movements as he cums. Alec's fingers dig into my hips, pressing into my soft flesh. I hope I'll have a little bruise, something to masturbate to.

After our orgasms subside, I pop off the vibrator and put it back into my purse. Alec pulls out slowly, careful to catch the condom hanging off his shrinking member. I straighten and pull my dress down with a shimmy. Alec looks down at me with a lazy smile.

"We should do this again," he says.

"Oh, yeah, totally," I tell him.

I tell him I'm going to pop away to the women's restroom to "freshen up." Instead, I push through the door to the employee exit and into the night.

Oceanside Pier is thriving at this time of night. It's a weekend, it's summer. High school kids skateboard near the amphitheater, while parents carry exhausted children covered in ice cream. I pass them all by, enjoying the summer air on my skin. It's almost chilly this time of night.

At the base of the pier sits a bunch of rocks. They're typically empty now, too dark to navigate without a flashlight. Plus, it's dangerous to be in these waters at night, riptides and all that. That's why I like this time best, there's no one to bother me. No one to perform for. I don't have to *be* anyone.

Not Addison the Boss.

Not Addison the Fuck Up.

Not Addison the Girl You Fucked In a Bathroom.

Just...me.

2

MELODY

When the moon crests, I slip away.

My sisters don't understand. They love the comfort and security of our family and ocean home. They love living in the depths, keeping the humans at a distance.

They remember the stories of our ancestors – of the men who stole our skin and held us hostage. Forced us to have children.

Stole us from the water.

This keeps them from shedding their skin as often as I do. They're happy to watch the lights of the city sparkle across the waves, winking at them from the pier.

I am not.

It is a beacon, and it calls me.

So, while they slumber, I wake and slip my skin. I

know where to hide it so the humans don't find it. I'm sure it is just a myth, these men who will steal our skin and force us to walk with them.

But I am careful anyway.

At first, the noise of the human world was too much. Bright and loud, crashing and thundering on my ears that only knew the water. With time I became accustomed to it, and now I stare into the lights on the boardwalk. I stand on the concrete and stare down at the band that plays, at the crowd that cheers.

My toes dig into the sand. My feet tear on the asphalt and sometimes bleed. They will heal once I put my skin back on, so I don't bother or worry.

Tonight, the air is cool, sending goose pimples along my exposed arms and back. Usually, it is too warm for me; I have grown used to the cold waters. Tonight is a perfect summer night.

I watch the smiling babies as they eat ice cream.

I clap at the men on the boards of skate – skate boards? Yes, skateboards. They are talented, jumping from obstacle to obstacle. When the Angry Men chase them away, I frown and boo. An Angry Man tries to threaten me and tells me to 'go home.'

Home. Hah.

I won't let him ruin my night. I continue down the boardwalk, to the streets, to the restaurants and the stores. I run my fingers through the beads with names on them. I try on a hat that's too big and laugh.

Eventually, I must go back.

Not 'home,' as the Angry Man said.

Back.

I take my time weaving through the thinning crowd of people and head to the sand, to the rocks where I've hidden my skin. It's always empty, the perfect place to conceal something as valuable as my skin.

Tonight is different – I can't find it. I check the rock I normally leave it tucked behind, then the one next to it, then the one next to that. I've covered the entire area until I realize something horrible.

My skin is gone.

3

ADDISON

The sound of crying is enough to disrupt anyone's buzz.

The rocks under the pier are typically peaceful this time of night - so peaceful that I can enjoy a glass of wine (or two or three) without seeing another soul. Sometimes the unhoused sleep down here, but mostly it's me, some kids macking on each other, and the waves.

Crying isn't typical.

At first, I ignore it.

If you ignore things, they go away. At least that's how I've treated a lot of things in my life. If I ignore the dripping faucet, eventually my roommates will call the landlord to fix it. If I ignore the trash piling up on the counter, eventually my roommates will throw it away.

If I ignore the reason I can't keep a steady job, relationship or … no, that's digging too deep.

No amount of ignoring stops the crying, which evolves into sad, hiccupping sobs. I know that feeling when you've cried yourself to emptiness. A part of my heart hurts for that sound, finds a mate in the gasping breaths. Another part of me, the part I let to the front too often, dismisses it.

Keep it together, Addison, we're in public. No tantrums no breakdowns.

Ugh, that voice again.

I pick my way down the rocks as quietly as I can. If I move quietly maybe I can avoid detection by the sobbing creature. It's probably some kid, crying over something that doesn't really matter. They'll forget in five to ten business days.

Or it'll haunt them forever. They'll be thirty years old, staring in the mirror as they put on their 50 SPF sunscreen and remember the time they cried under the Oceanside pier.

Tragic.

Almost as tragic as my foot slipping and me sliding down the rock in my dress, landing loudly in the shallow water. The crying stops immediately, and suddenly there's a face looking down at me. It's tear-stained and beautiful – in a tragic way. Her eyes are big and wide, red-rimmed from her tears. They remind me a bit of the seals at La Jolla, the way they're perfectly circular and filled with a curious kindness. She has long thin blonde hair that falls over her face, mirroring it like a sunburst.

"Are you okay?" she asks in an unplaceable accent. Her voice is low, gravely, like there's sand in her throat. She was just crying for an unknown amount of time; I guess my voice would go through the wringer, too.

"Yeah, just a little fall," I tell her, standing and brushing the sand off my dress. "But don't worry about me, I'll just be..." I start to say, trying to move away from her.

"How long have you been here?" she asks.

She doesn't move away from me as I stand, preferring to keep painfully close to me. I hate rude people who crowd me, all up in my personal space. My general rule is that if I can smell you, you need to take a step back. I miss the early days of COVID – not because I like the idea of a terrible disease taking over the planet, but because everyone stayed six feet from me. It was wonderful. Now everyone is back to shoving themselves together, either out of habit or to be an asshole.

But her closeness isn't unnerving. Maybe it's because she's beautiful and I'm shallow.

"Uh, on planet Earth? In California?" I ask for clarification because both sound like reasonable assumptions.

"On the rocks," she says – which makes more sense

than my line of thought. She doesn't sound at all peeved by my wrong assumption, which is a welcome change. Typically, people think I'm intentionally being an asshole when I ask for clarification.

On the rocks. Like a martini.

"Uh, a few hours. Maybe. I'm not sure, honestly. Why?"

"I lost something. I left it here for safekeeping, but it was gone when I came back," she says. She sounds dejected by this, as though leaving something valuable on a crowded beach during peak tourist season wasn't a recipe for disaster. I try not to let my eyebrows climb too far up my forehead.

"Was it worth a lot?" I ask.

"Yes," she says with a heavy sigh, sitting down on the sand. She draws her knees to her chest and hugs them. She doesn't care that her white shorts are about to be ruined, but she's not wearing shoes so maybe she's one of those people. You know, the ones who move to the beach for a few months – live in a van, don't wear shoes, think showering is a suggestion.

"Huh, well. Sorry?"

"Did you see anyone come or go?" she presses, looking up at me.

"I mean, yes. Kinda. There were people who came and went, but I wasn't keeping a close eye. Did they take something really big?" I try to think back but my short-term memory is like a goldfish when it comes to things that don't directly involve me.

"My skin," she says softly. "They took my skin."

I take another look at her. She's not very young, not like the youth with their *rizz* and their *no cap* and such. I hadn't heard *skin*, but then again where would I? I'm pushing thirty, I'm a data analyst, and my roommates are all in their thirties trying to make ends meet. I'm not exactly surrounded by kids these days.

"Is that like, a metaphor?" I ask.

"No. I need it to get home, though. Without it...I'm stuck here," she opens her arms to the sand, the beach.

Maybe it's some new bag? Don't they make nicknames for all the cool items now? Like those giant drink containers, they have some name I cannot for the life of me remember right now. The metal ones that double as weapons? The girl in accounting has so many I lose track of the colors. Every day it's like a game – what color is her drink container today? I tried to rope some of my coworkers into it with me, they think the game is cruel.

Maybe a skin is a bag, with her keys. Or it's a wallet.

"Damn," I say, inching away. She says nothing, her large eyes trained on the water as it rolls in and laps at the shore. She looks so sad, and I guess I would be too if I were stranded.

Maybe it's the wine, or that part of me that understands her tears win out.

"So do you need help looking for it?" I hear myself say. The words are barely out of my mouth before I regret them. Still, I continue. "I can help you look around for a bit. But it's getting late, so we don't have much time before they consider it loitering and kick us out."

Bright light breaks across her face, and my heart stutters to a stop. Displaced of its agony she is a beacon of light, her smile spread and stretched over her face. Thank god for the darkness, it hides the blush that spreads across my face. I've never had someone look at me like that. It hits my stomach like a punch to the gut.

"You'd do that?" she asks breathlessly. She unfurls her limbs to stand, her smile still a thousand watts as she turns it on me.

"Yeah, I mean...I'd want someone to do that for me, you know?" I say because I mean it. If someone reached a hand out to me when I was down, my life might have turned out differently. Imagining someone being kind to me has my stomach turning over again.

"I owe you my thanks and my life," she says.

"That's a little dramatic," I say, but she's not offended.

She just laughs. "I'm Melody," she says.

"Addison," I return.

She nods, and we begin the search amongst the rocks. It's a logical place to start, the last place Melody saw her skin or whatever. We turn each one over, and the ones too heavy to lift we adjust as best we can.

An hour creeps by and there's no sign of her skin.

"Where are you staying?" I ask. Maybe I'll walk her back to her place, and make sure she gets home safe. Then tomorrow she can meet up with her friends or family or whoever she's staying with and it'll become their problem.

I've done my good deed.

"I guess here," she says, looking around the rocks.

"Where's home?" I ask. She glances out to the ocean and then back to me. The light from the board-walk catches her eyes and they're shiny with tears again.

"I can't get there without my skin," she affirms.

"There's no one who can let you in?" Skin must be a wallet, then. Or a purse. I guess a purse or a wallet would have her key card or her key or whatever.

She shakes her head and sits in the sand again, burying her face in her knees. I want to reach out and put a hand on her shoulder, but that is so invasive. I also want to wrap my arms around her and pull her close, to tell her that she's not alone.

That's even more invasive, and it's a lie. She is alone.

"Why don't you stay with me?" I ask. My word vomit is out of control today. Her head jerks up from her knobby knees, her bright gaze meeting mine. The look in them – the hope, the adoration – makes my heart skip a beat. No one has ever looked at me like that. I'm used to eye rolls or disgusted looks. Melody looks at me like I'm some sort of savior.

"You mean it?" she asks, her voice soft.

I nod. I have to glance away, or I'm going to drown in her wide, brown eyes. "Yeah, I mean I have a couch, it's no big deal. We'll reunite you with your friends or whatever tomorrow."

Melody stands and shakes the sand from her. She reaches out to brush her fingers along my arm before pulling me into a hug. It nearly shatters my bones. Her breath is hot on my ear as she says, "Thank you. You're amazing."

Before I can say anything stupid, she pulls back and I have no choice but to lead a shoeless stranger to my house.

4
____

MELODY

This human lives in a community, much like I do.

I've always wondered about the lives of the humans; it's why I was so drawn to the pier to begin with. The lights, the smells, the sounds - it's all so much brighter than underwater. When I am in my skin and a selkie, these things are different. Colors are not the same, sensations like water or heat don't register the same. Even my taste is altered.

I follow the human, Addison, through the streets which are empty now. The pier closed a while ago, and I'm not sure how long I looked for my skin, but it must have been a long time. The people who walk the streets are wisps of kelp – floating in the sways, letting it take them wherever it may lead. They are aimless, unlike Addison and me.

She takes me to a small house. Inside is a land creature, one I recognize as a cat. It watches me with its wide pupils, able to see as well at night as I am. Addison catches me watching the cat as she flips on the light inside the home, temporarily blinding me in the process.

"That's Garbage," she says. "I tell people it's like the 90's female rock band, but really it's because she was found in the garbage. Emilio is a softie," she adds. Her voice is pitched low, quiet so as not to wake her community.

"She is very pretty," I say, taking a step toward the cat.

"Oh, she's not friendly," Addison says, her voice raising in warning.

But I am not afraid of Garbage, I can read her signals. She is just as curious about me as I am about her. I must smell like the outdoors she was born into, and the food she craves. I've met many a cat on the docks and the shore; they are solitary creatures – so opposite of selkies.

Garbage sniffs my hand tentatively, then pushes the side of her face into it. Scent for scent.

"Wow, okay," Addison says, her tone offended. "It took like...months for Garbage to stop hissing at me."

"I'm sure it wasn't you," I tell Addison because she is giving me a place to stay. She offered to help find my skin. I should be kind to her in return since I have nothing to pay her back with yet.

Addison says nothing and leads me through the quiet house to a room. It is small, with a bed against the wall, a dresser that is covered with drinking cups, and a small sofa against the opposite wall. The closet has no door, and clothes spill from it onto the floor of the room.

"Sorry it's a mess," she says, shoveling her clothes into the closet with her foot. "If you're okay with the couch," she says, pointing to the sofa. "Otherwise, it's the floor."

"Thank you," I say as I sit on the couch. It's old and sinks in the middle, but it's better than the sand. I once fell asleep under the pier and woke up to angry people yelling at me, saying I can't sleep on the beach. Not like the Angry Man, but close – different uniform. Still very angry.

"The bathroom is through that door – I don't share with anyone, so you won't have to worry about being walked in on," she says, nodding to a door near the sofa. "If you need to...brush your teeth or whatever there's an extra toothbrush in the cabinet."

When I say nothing, Addison gathers her things and disappears into the bathroom. I look around the room once more, taking in the unmade bed, the half-full cups on the dresser, and the nightstand that's missing a leg. I like this, this random assortment of items. She is a collector of mismatched things. My own room back home is like this, though I have to hide my trinkets. If my family knew how much I took from the humans they'd never let me out of their sight again.

When she leaves the bathroom, she's wearing shorts that accentuate her backside. I try not to look, but I'm drawn to the way her rounded flesh peeks from it. I resist the urge to reach out and touch, as that would be strange. We are not at a level of intimacy that allows touch, especially with how she reacted to my hug. I snap my attention to the bathroom door until Addison hands me something.

"Here," she says. "You can't sleep in that, it's filthy."

She's talking about my borrowed clothes. I found them after I realized being naked was not tolerated in the human world. It should have made sense – I wear my skin when I'm in the water, I need new skin when I'm on land. My clothes are a mix of things from the stores on the shore and items I found outside a donation place. I don't have any money, so I had to borrow them...but I'm not sure when or if I'll ever return them.

"Thank you," I say as I take the clothes she hands me. I start to change right away, but then remember that Addison went into the bathroom to do so. It is not common for humans to change in front of each other; I know this from experience. I shuffle into the bathroom and put on her clothes. They are comfortable – a large T-shirt that drapes down to my knees, and a pair of soft shorts with words on the backside that are faded. I turn on the faucet and rinse my face, trying to remove the tracks of saltwater tears from earlier.

Don't cry, Melody. You got yourself into this mess, you can get yourself out.

Yes, the mess I was always warned about. A human took my skin, and they can use it to marry me and keep me on shore against my will. I'm not ready to have children. I think I'm ready to be married, but I would have liked to meet them in a better circumstance. The other selkies are not to my liking – not romantically anyway.

Perhaps I just misplaced it – wrong pier, wrong rocks. It isn't possible, but I think them to soothe myself. If I can keep a smile on my face and my hopes up anything can happen.

So, I smile at myself in the mirror and leave the bathroom. The sofa is set up with blankets and a pillow. Addison sits at the end of her bed, holding a cup of water in her hands. "Here," she says, handing it to me. "You must be thirsty."

I was, so I drink it all and hand it back to her. She places it on her dresser with all the other cups and laughs. "I guess I should clean that tomorrow."

"After we search for my skin some more?" I ask.

Addison nods and crawls into bed, pulling the

covers up to hide her body. She leans over to flip the light switch off, plunging the room into darkness. I watch her for a minute before I settle into the sofa and pull my covers over me, falling asleep in a human's home for the first time.

5

ADDISON

The sun is high in the sky by the time Melody gives up at the pier. She woke me up at first light, even though we didn't go to bed until nearly 1 am. She was so polite about it, making a series of light coughs and movements until I opened my eyes.

Polite, but annoying. I require at least 8-10 hours of sleep a night to be considered a functioning human being. Apparently, Melody is built on something different – she is bright-eyed and bushy-tailed for our morning adventure, then takes a short 10-minute nap in the afternoon sun, then is ready to go again.

It's exhausting.

We start at the scene of the crime - the pier. I ask her multiple times what this skin looks like - how big it is, what color it is, etc. Her responses are incomprehensible.

How big is it? *My size.*

What color is it? *Skin colored - gray, spotted a bit.*

What's it made of? *Skin.*

With little to go on I'm stuck following after her, picking up rocks and peering under them. She shakes her head when I do, reminding me that it is too large to be found under a rock. She is laughing, and at first, so am I. But then the sun climbs higher, she takes a nap, and we've run out of options.

"I think someone may have stolen it," I tell her as gently as I can. I'm not sure how she'll take this – Melody is not predictable. At first, I thought she was simple, but the more I get to know her, the more I realize she's an eternal optimist. Her tears from last night are long gone, replaced with a beaming smile. I feel bad for her – once she realizes someone stole her skin, she's going to be heartbroken.

"I presume so, yes," she agrees lightly. "I was warned," she tells me.

Of course she was, there are signs all up and down the beach and the parking areas about theft. Don't leave valuables in your car, don't leave shit unlocked, the usual. I've seen Melody read, so I can only assume she was aware of the possibility when leaving something so valuable in a bunch of rocks under the pier.

"So you could file a police report?" I suggest.

She chews her lip, the first moment of uncertainty

she's given since we started looking this morning. "I'm not sure I want them involved," she says carefully.

Now I'm intrigued. What is *in* this skin? There's no way this woman is involved in any sort of crime, she'd be eaten alive! She's just a hair over five feet tall with knobby knees and sharp elbows. Sure, I watch too many murder shows, but Melody doesn't fill the bill of a criminal. A patsy? Absolutely.

"Okay, how about posters?" I ask. She shakes her head, adjusting the oversized sunglasses on her face as they slip. We had to buy them for her because she kept squinting and covering her eyes against the sun like some pothead.

"This is...delicate," she says, her hands reaching out to grab mine. It's an intimate gesture, far too intimate for someone I've known less than twenty-four hours. I don't pull back, instead, I marvel at the feel of her hands on mine. The pads of my fingers are rough from typing, hers are soft, callous-free. I expected them to be dry and cracked from living on the beach.

I have to force my eyes up to hers to pay attention because the sensation of her skin on mine is making my brain dip into longing. This is where my mind goes when I find an attractive guy in a bar. This is pre-fuck-in-the-bathroom-Addison. Melody is too...I don't know, she doesn't come off as the type of woman you can throw up against a bathroom wall and then walk away from. She also knows where I live.

"You see, no one is supposed to know about the skin. About me, either. If my family found out, I'd be in huge trouble," she tells me. Now I'm concerned *for* her.

"Melody," I tell her softly, my gaze darting around to make sure no one is too close to overhear. I step towards her, wanting her body safely close to me. "If you're in trouble, I can help you." I don't recognize this knightess in shining armor.

The things I do for pretty people. But it's more than that – I want to see that smile from last night again.

"You are helping me," she says with another thousand-watt smile. There it is.

"Okay, if you say so," I reply. I want to dig deeper into this subject – her family, the one that would get her in trouble for losing something. Something so valuable she'd cry over its loss, something so secret she couldn't make posters or tell the police.

"Is there a time limit on this operation?" I asked her.

She sighs and lets go of my left hand – just the left one. The right is still firmly in hers, palms pressed together, fingers slipping between mine. She's holding my hand like a fucking middle school crush.

And like a fucking middle schooler, it thrills me.

"I think I have a few days before they notice I'm gone," she confirms.

Okay, so clearly not that type of cult, the type who keeps constant dibs. She is a grown woman; she has to be my age if not older. She's on her own enough to slip away for a few days, but not so alone that someone wouldn't notice her absence.

Would anyone notice if I went missing? How many days would I need to be gone for someone to care? *Too many.* Don't they say the first forty-eight hours are the most important? Yeah, it'd take at least a week or two before anyone realized anything. My work would assume I flaked – I'm a new hire with a sketchy employment history. My roommates wouldn't notice unless I skipped on rent, or if I started to smell. Garbage would probably eat me well before anyone else realized I was dead.

I snap out of that macabre thought as Melody's fingers tighten against mine. "Where did you go?" she asks. I can't see her eyes behind the ridiculous sunglasses we bought for her, but I assume they're as wide and expressive as always. The woman peers into my soul, I swear.

"I was just thinking," I say dismissively. "You hungry?"

We sit outside my favorite Mexican joint. She gets a fish taco, I get a chicken one. For a while, we are silent, which is new for me. I hate silence, I hate the awkward way it sits on my skin. There's nothing comfortable about it. I struggle to think of something to fill the void.

"What were you thinking about?" Melody asks. It's been over ten minutes since we last spoke, I'm surprised she's still stuck on it. She picks the pieces of fish from the tortilla and tosses them into her mouth. She should have gotten a fish bowl, not a taco.

"I don't remember," I lie. Typically, when I tell people what I've been thinking it leads to some awkward moments. She knows I'm lying; I can tell by the look she gives me over her sunglasses. I sigh. "Fine. I was thinking – you said it would take a few days before someone noticed you were gone, and I wondered how long it would take anyone to notice I was missing."

"And?" she asks.

"It's more than a few days," I say. "I mean, it depends on the time of the month. If rent is due soon, then my roommates would notice that I didn't pay and that they can't find me. My work – probably a day or two and someone would call my cellphone, which I wouldn't answer. See, in this scenario, I'm dead, or kidnapped. So I wouldn't have my cellphone, therefore I wouldn't answer. They'd think I flaked and drop it. If it's right after I paid rent, and I was dead in my bath-room – like I fell and hit my head – I think as long as it would take to start to smell. In the winter, maybe a bit longer. In the summer, with humidity? Not so long. Garbage would eat me, definitely." I shove a large piece of the taco in my mouth to stop myself from yammering on.

"Hmm," she says thoughtfully, chewing thoughtfully on the last piece of fish. To her credit she didn't go through a face journey of shock to concern to 'get me the hell out of here' like most people do. I tell them at least once where my mind was, so they don't ask again. Usually, I pick something a little less severe than my death and disappearance.

"What about your family?" she asks.

"What about my family?"

"How long until they notice you're gone?"

I shrug. "We're not close. My dad's dead, my mom has her own life across the country. We catch up a few times a year, but not often enough for her to notice I'm gone. Not like your family, I suppose," I add.

She frowns a little at this. "My family just wants what's best for me. Our ancestors have gone through tough times and have been in tough situations. They know being here, losing my skin – it's dangerous. I may become like them."

I may become like them. I understand that all too well. My mom never knew what she wanted out of life. She didn't want a kid – but didn't *not* want a kid either – so when she got pregnant she kept me. She liked my dad well enough, they got married – it wasn't loveless, but they weren't in love either. I don't want to become like them, and I don't think my mom does either.

She also didn't want this life for me, so I guess there are wins and losses in the game of life.

"Why won't they let you back without this skin?" I ask.

"I can't get to them without it. If I don't have it, I can't physically get home," she says.

"You can't, like...have a copy made?"

"Of what?"

"The skin. You don't have a backup copy of it?"

"That's not how it works. I have one skin, just like you have one skin."

"Well, technically, our skin is made up of a lot of skin cells. And those skin cells fall off and die all the time – it's what dust is made of. It's just dead skin, sloshing about the air. So really we don't have one skin, we have a lot of skin, that turns over and over..." I trail off, but I've run out of food to shove into my mouth.

"Really?" she says, leaning forward, fascinated. "So your skin – you take it off all the time?"

"Well, I guess. Yeah. Slowly, over time. I've probably lost a decent chunk of it since we've met," I say.

She nods and smiles to herself. "You lose your skin to the world, but the world does not take you or keep you. You are still you, you are still Addison." She pops another piece of fish in her mouth, satisfied.

6

MELODY

The sun sets and my skin is still missing.

Addison is right – someone took it. I don't know why someone would do that (*your ancestors warned you they knew this would happen and you ignored it you…*)

Perhaps they thought it was a dead seal, or perhaps they thought it was too valuable to stay on the beach. Maybe I should listen to Addison and we should get the Angry Men involved in this. If someone brought it to their station they might be holding it. I couldn't go to the station, though – they'd ask questions. They'd want identification. They'd want answers I couldn't give them.

Unlike Addison, whom I've already told so much. I don't know any other humans the way I do Addison. She is so easy to talk to, and when I tell her things, she thinks about them for a long time. I watch her thoughts move across her face, jumping from start to finish before she speaks.

"Maybe we should involve the police," I say as we walk along the beach. It's emptying now that the sunset is over. I marvel at the colors as they dance across the ocean, so different at this angle. I'm used to seeing it from the surface of the waves.

"Yeah?" Addison asks, surprised. We hadn't spoken much over the last few minutes, meandered along the beach, her sweaty palm pressed into mine. I like holding her hand – I've seen other humans do it on the pier. It's a sign of closeness, of friendship. I suspect it's also a sign of courting. I wouldn't be against that; Addison is very pretty. I want to make sure she's not being nice to me out of pity, I don't think my heart could take that.

I stop and turn to her, watching the way the final rays of sun light her face. Her green eyes remind me of the ocean plants near where my family sleeps, and her red hair billows around her face in the breeze. I want to run my fingers through it. The sight of her like this catches the words in my throat and I have to swallow before I speak again. "Maybe someone brought it to them, and they're holding it," I tell her.

"Would they do that?" Addison asks. She's watching me closely, her gaze darting from my eyes to my lips. I wet them with my tongue and watch her gaze linger a bit longer, her fingers tighten against mine.

"Maybe," I admit. "I hope so – I don't like the idea of someone else wearing it."

"What does it look like?" Addison asks.

She's tried this before, the line of questioning to determine what my skin looks like. I suppose it's only fair I tell her now; we are no longer strangers. I slept in her room, she fed me, we're holding hands. This is a level of closeness I feel comfortable telling her about my true nature.

"It is a seal skin – I'm a selkie," I tell her.

She blinks, a slow movement compared to the thoughts rocketing across her face. I watch them all, knowing this could happen. The ancestors warned us about this as well – disbelief. If you tell the wrong person, they separate you from your skin forever and put you somewhere far from the water with locks on the doors and windows.

Without water, we die.

Without our skin, we die.

"A selfie?" she asks for clarity. I'm not familiar with this word, but it does sound similar to the human name for my kind.

"Selkie," I correct. "My skin is that of a seal – I take it off when I want to come onto land." I stop short of saying *and be with humans*, because once I clarify that I am *other* she'll think about this too hard.

"Okay, so your skin is...a seal? Like a live one?" Her gaze flickers like it does when she goes away, when her mind is moving through more thoughts than it can hold. I've watched her do it a few times, how she can't listen to what I say until she's landed on a conclusion.

I wait patiently until her eyes settle. "It's not alive until it's on me, I guess. Without me it's just skin. With me, we are one," I tell her. I wish I could feel it, I wish I had a connection to it. A beacon that guided me to know where it is. But when I'm in my human form my senses are dulled, and the skin is nothing more than a shell.

"Is it...sentient?" she asks.

I shake my head. "No, it's like..." What is something that is not alive until it is a part of you?

"Hair?" I offer. She tilts her head at this.

"So someone else could wear your skin?"

"No," I reply, horrified. The skin is mine – I was born in it, I'll likely die in it. Someone else touching it is enough to make me feel like I've fallen under a great wave, unable to swim to the surface. Someone else *wearing* it...

I think she sees this on my face because she quickly changes the subject. "So if we go to the police station we ask if...anyone's turned in seal skin?"

"Yes, but I can't come with," I say, glad for the change. For all her daydreaming she's very observant, I like that about her. I also like when she says her thoughts aloud, and I can follow how they connect from one idea to the next.

"Why not?" she asks. "Are you worried about your family getting there first?"

I shake my head. "No, they wouldn't dare travel this far on land. The police will want...records. Proof. They'll want to know who I am," I tell her.

"And you don't have any ID because of your family?" she guesses.

I shake my head, then pause. "Yes, but no. We don't exist, as far as this world knows. We are myths, from a time long ago."

This must unsettle her because she stares at me long and hard before nodding. "Okay – I can go to the police for you. But I need to know more about your family, more about your skin."

So I tell her everything over dinner.

Addison is a very good listener.

7

———

ADDISON

Melody is a wonderful storyteller.

We sit on the concrete steps near the pier. She's eating fish – again – while I enjoy a hot dog. She sits cross-legged, wolfing down the fish. I'm not sure it's fully cooked, but she doesn't seem to care. She doesn't even spit out the bones I hear crunch between her teeth.

"See, when we take our skin off, we can walk on the land," she tells me between mouthfuls. "Otherwise, we are like seals, swimming in the waters. Some of us live in pods far away from the shore, others like to stay close. In the past, our kind has been mistreated, and some of us remember warnings from our ancestors."

"What kind of warnings?" I manage to get in.

This is the first time she hesitates, looking down at

her food for a long moment. "Just that some people take advantage of you, that's all."

"That's a hard lesson to learn," I agree. "But everyone takes advantage of everyone – that's not unique to you or your family," I tell her. I need her to see that her family has given her unrealistic fears about the world. Everyone has the capacity for harm. In fact, most people *will* harm if they could. Kindness is not the way of the world. Her family isn't wrong, but I still tread lightly.

"Yes, but not in this way," she tells me, before continuing with her story as though I didn't interrupt.

"I've been warned by my family about spending too much time on land. Some of us come to land when we're ready to mate. That's not what I was doing, though. I told them that was the case. Really, I just...I wanted to see this world. The lights of the pier are so inviting, and I love the sounds and the lights. It's always so exciting.

"They caught on, though. They knew my trips here were not to find a mate, because I never came back with one. Not even a courtship. So, they tried to keep me away, but I just became sneakier." She smiles at this, and I understand that streak of rebellion. When your parents tell you no, you find your yes. Mine was to run away across the country to a state I'd only seen on TV.

"I'm very careful at hiding my skin. I can see better in the dark than you can, so I keep it someplace very special. I guess I've grown lazy because when I returned my skin was gone. Until I find it, I can't return to the water. I'm stuck here on land, destined to..." she trails off, chewing her lip rapidly. "Whoever has my skin, can force me to stay here. If I get it back from them, I'm free."

I almost believe Melody. She speaks with total conviction, presenting everything as a fact. I half expect to look into the water and see large seal eyes staring up at me, knowing that I'm harboring one of their own.

"Are all seals selkies?" I ask, suddenly uncomfortable by the thought. Aquariums come to mind first.

"No, but all selkies have seal skin," she says. I smile at the alteration – Melody makes musical memories by the Monterey...moat? No, there's no moat here, and we're not in Monterey. "What?" she asks when I smile.

"Oh – you know, all selkies have seal skin. Kind of like, Sally sells seashells by the seashore," I tell her. "It's a bit of a tongue twister."

"It is," she agrees, and doesn't look at all upset by my change of subject. If anything she's enamored by it, whispering the words quietly under her breath. *Sally sells seashells by the seashore...*

"So, if you don't ever find your skin, what then? You're stuck here?" I ask.

Her smile drops and I instantly regret it. I don't mean to; I can't help but jump to the worst conclusion at any given point or time. I'm a storm cloud, always raining on everyone else. It's not my fault they don't think through every possible bad scenario and prepare for it. I can't stop my mind from doing so.

"I am – stuck to the one who has my skin. It's how they keep us here. I didn't want to tell you, but I don't think you'd do that to me," she adds. "I think the warnings from the ancestors are about different sorts of people. People who take advantage, who are selfish. You're none of those."

I'm not sure how she came to that conclusion, because I am all those things. I think of myself first because no one else will. I take advantage because there's no other way to stay alive. This world is so different from hers, I'm afraid that if she stays here much longer that bright bulb will burn out. Reality is the ultimate buzzkill.

"I'm glad you think that," I tell her. I want to add *but I'm not I'm all of the things your family warns you about, I'm sad and lonely and depressed and selfish and if I found your skin first, I'd probably ask for money for it.*

She turns her attention to the water, scooting close to me now that her food is gone. The sun set over an hour ago, and the lights of the boats twinkle on the horizon. Melody leans her head on my shoulder, her hair tickling my ear.

I don't move, afraid that if I so much as breathe too loud, she'll move away.

I can't think about that without feeling sad.

8

MELODY

Addison is a fitful sleeper.

I prefer to take multiple naps throughout the day, but humans don't do that. I only got a few naps today, so when I settle back onto the couch in her bedroom, I'm very tired. I'm not sure how long I sleep, but when I wake it's because she's tossing and turning. It's like her dreams are waves that pull her under, clogging her mouth and nose with water.

I slip from the sofa and stand near the edge of her bed, listening. She's speaking, but the words don't make any sense. I lean closer, trying to keep my hair from touching her arm. I'm afraid she'll wake up and scream or associate me with whatever is bad in her dreams.

I don't want that.

I lift the edge of her covers and slip under them,

sliding my body until I'm near her. She tosses again, her mouth turned down in an angry frown. "You lied," she whispers in her sleep, her voice choked. "You promised…"

I wrap my arms around her, pulling her tight into me. I'm the shell to her snail, I'm the house that will protect her from the waves. She tightens in my grip, her muscles rigid at the new sensation. I wonder if anyone has held her like this before, soothed the ache from her body.

"Melody?" she asks softly. Her eyelashes brush against my neck, where I'm holding her tightly to me. They're wet with tears.

"You were dreaming. Nightmares," I tell her, not loosening my grip. She doesn't fight me, but she is still tense in my arms. I worry that she doesn't want me to, that this closeness is making it worse. "I'm sorry, I didn't mean to wake you," I start. I should crawl out of her bed and into the street, far away from her. She's already given me so much help that I cannot return. And now I forced myself into her bed, forced closeness she didn't ask for. Just because I want to be near her doesn't mean she wants to be near me.

"I'm glad you did," she says. Slowly, as if prying open a particularly tough clamshell, she relaxes. Each muscle, one at a time, unraveling in my arms.

"Really?" I ask. "Are you sure? I can…" I trail off. *I can leave. I can go.*

"Please..." She doesn't finish.

Please stay? Please go? Please don't go? Please what what what?

Her hands move along my body, her fingers tracing along my delicate human skin. I feel fire in their wake, heat like a summer day trailing where her fingers are. My breath catches and I'm drowning, my lungs full of water.

But I don't want it to stop.

Her fingers slow after a while, her breath following suit. She is no longer rigid in my arms as sleep claims her again.

I want to wake her up again, to feel her fingers trail the foreign landscape of this human skin. I want to learn it with her, I want to know if she feels this good everywhere else. I want so many things from this human, things that make my chest tight and my body ache. I'd give her my skin in exchange for another touch.

Instead, I hold her close, memorizing the feel of her breath on my neck, the way she smells like sweat and salt air and something else I can't place.

I hold her until morning, so she's not alone with the nightmares.

9

———

ADDISON

elody's soft breaths tickle the hair on my forehead. I resist every temptation to shift, to move, to show that I'm awake because I don't want her to let me go. She heard my nightmares and didn't turn away. In fact, she turned towards me – crawling off the couch and into bed with me.

She must know I'm awake because she shifts slightly, and I'm too slow to suppress my groan. I don't want her to move away, but I'm painfully aware that her arm is probably asleep and she likely has to pee. The sun filtering through the window tells me it's mid-morning, who knows how long she's been awake, unmoving.

To my surprise – and happiness – she doesn't untangle herself from me. The fingers of her left-hand trail over my shoulder, sending pleasant goosebumps in their wake.

"No more nightmares?" she asks, her voice rough from sleep.

I shake my head, still unwilling to open my eyes. Her fingers slide up my shoulder to my neck, then my chin, tilting my head back to gaze up at her. When I blink them open, she's framed in the hazy morning light, looking like some sort of goddess.

"Good," she says, her gaze flickering to my lips.

I want her, I realize. I want her in a way that is more than a quick fuck in a bathroom or a month-long crash and burn. My brain can't comprehend what that means so I settle for this thought: I want to wake up with her tomorrow, and the day after, and the day after.

Would kissing her be wrong?

She crawled into my bed and held me in my sleep. She grabbed my hand yesterday, rested her head on my shoulder. These are not the motions of someone who is just tolerating me. These aren't mixed signals.

Still, I worry – am I taking advantage of her? She thinks she's a mythical creature searching for her skin!

Does being in some weird cult make her unable to make her own decisions?

C'mon, Addison – think this through. She's a grown-ass woman, she just has a weird family. Who doesn't?

My brain races and she watches it, her wide eyes thoughtful.

"What are you thinking?" she asks, her voice just above a whisper.

I lick my lips because I want to tell her how I feel. She didn't turn away from my racing thoughts yesterday...but this is different. Maybe in her cult, this closeness is normal and I'm overthinking what she considers simple friendship?

"Do you need help, Melody?" I ask, unable to voice my deeper thoughts.

"Help?" she echoes.

"Yeah, did you...did you run away from your family? Do you need help?" I clarify.

She frowns a little and I hate the sight of it on her face. I want her to smile again, I don't want to be the reason she's not.

"No, I am free to do as I wish. If I wanted to come to land and live amongst you, I could. They'd be sad, but they'd understand. It's not unheard of," she tells me.

"But you can't return to them without your...skin," I press.

"Physically, yes. There's no way this body would be able to live where we do, I need my skin to get there." Her gaze roves my face as she speaks. "Why are you asking this? Is this really what you were thinking?"

"No," I admit. "Not really. I mean...I just want to make sure you know what you're doing. That you don't need more help than I can offer. The thing with the police, it got me worried about your family."

"They just want me to be happy," she says, her gaze darting back to my lips. "This is what you were thinking about as I hold you? My family?"

"No," I breathe.

"No?" she echoes, her lips quirking in a teasing smile. She knows what I'm thinking.

Then her lips press against mine. There's no hesitation, no questioning – where I am a fumbling mess, she is assured, patient.

The kiss starts chaste – her soft lips on mine, her fingers trailing along my jaw in encouragement. She takes her time, kissing my top lip then my bottom, waiting for me to relax. I can't – my mind is in a tailspin of want. If this goes poorly, I will be devastated, and that makes this all so much harder.

She flicks her tongue against my lips, begging me to open my mouth to her. I do, sucking in a breath at the feel of her softness against me. This is no hurried kiss on the dance floor, this is slow, luxurious. Melody is patient as she tastes my lips, my mouth, my tongue.

Her hand trails from my jaw down my neck, feeling along the exposed skin. I shiver against her as my mind spirals.

She kissed you, that means she likes you. You weren't reading into things.

She's going to leave the minute she finds that damn skin.

If the skin if even real, that is. It could be made up.

Why would someone make up losing a skin? Why would someone pretend to be a selkie?

So, what – she is a selkie now? She's some mythical creature that spends half her life as a seal?

Well, more than half her life. If she's barely on shore...

"Stop," she says, pausing her kiss.

I jerk back, hit by her words. I should have known better; I *was* taking advantage of her. She may have started the kiss, but I should have stopped it before it got this far.

"You're not here with me," she accuses. "I want you here, not...elsewhere."

"I can't help it," I admit, my face flushing. How did she know that I'd zoned out? Did I stop kissing her? Oh god, do I do that every time I zone out?

"I want you here," she repeats, her hand reaching for me again. Her touch grazes my hip where my shirt has ridden up, exposing skin. Her cool hands bring awareness to how hot my skin is.

"I'll try," I offer, but it's a lost cause. Keeping my mind quiet for even a second has never been my strong point. This situation doesn't help - this rollercoaster of emotions I'm feeling isn't made any easier by her eagerness.

"Hmm," she says, because it's clear she doesn't believe me. Her wide eyes take me in, watching my face. I focus as hard as I can on her, the guilt rising as my errant grocery list threatens to take over my limited focus. If not the grocery list, then the chores...

"Do you..." she starts, then sighs. "I'm sorry, if this is not what you wanted." She starts to move from the bed and my heart shatters.

"No, wait. No, that's not it – at all. I do...I think."

"You think?" she asks. She is skeptical, but at least she stops moving.

I exhale a loud breath before continuing. "I've just...are you sure? Are you sure that you want me, you want to...kiss me, and hold my hand?"

"Yes, of course. That's why I did it," she says simply, as if it were that easy. As if this were all that easy. She believes she's a selkie, she's in my bed kissing me, and she'll be gone the minute she finds her skin. Back to her family, or the ocean, or wherever it is she lives. "Are you sure that you want *me*? You're okay with kissing me and holding my hand?" she counters.

"Yes," I say, surprised at how easily the answer comes. That is what I want, she is what I want.

"Good," she says, and her lips are on mine again. Conversation over, case closed.

This time, though, she's more insistent. She draws my bottom lip into her mouth, her teeth gently raking it before she lets it go with a pop. Her hand presses into my hip, pulling me against her, erasing the distance she created.

Her increased pace helps because I can focus more entirely on her. She's everywhere on me, her lips against mine, her breast against my chest, her fingers on my hips. Her nails trace lightly on the exposed flesh of my lower abdomen, sending a pleasant shiver along my spine. I groan into her mouth, and her lips quirk in a smile against mine.

She flips me onto my back, a knee on either side of my hips. Melody pushes my shirt up over my head, exposing my breasts to the cool room air. My nipples pebble immediately, and I'm not sure if it's from the cold air or the way her gaze locks on them. She pauses, my shirt still in her hands, then grins down at me. Her lips are red and swollen from our kissing.

"What?" I ask.

"I want to try something," she says.

"Okayyyyy," I reply. I want to try her lips on my body, but I keep that to myself.

"Do you have…" She mimics something over her ears with her hands.

"Headphones? Earplugs? Ear muffs? A hat?"

"Yes!" she says, snapping her fingers.

Helpful.

"The top drawer of my dresser," I say, nodding to it. I groan at the loss of the weight of her on my hips. I resist the urge to touch myself in her absence, wanting friction.

"Close your eyes," she says, her back to me. I obey and wait. Her weight returns to the bed, the edge of it sinking under her as she crawls back over me. Her fingers slide along my neck to my jaw, then she's placed something over my eyes. I open my eyes, seeing only the dark material of my shirt. Next, she slides head-phones over my ears, keeping the blindfold in place and blocking out any sound.

"For the distraction," she says into my neck, her words a rumbling vibration up my skin. It's not perfect, there's some light around the edges, and I can hear if she's close to me. My other senses flare, trying to compensate for the dulling of my vision and hearing.

All I can focus on is her lips and tongue as they trace their way down my neck, to my collarbone. Her teeth dig into my skin, and I jump under her touch. I feel more than hear her chuckle in response. She jour-neys downward to my breast, taking a nipple in her mouth with surprising delicacy. Her tongue flicks against it and it rises to attention. I squeeze my thighs together, trying to angle my hips so the seam of my shorts rubs my clit.

Melody's nails dig into the soft skin of my lower abdomen, and I jump again, this time with a whimper. I can't hear what she says in return, but it sounds an awful lot like 'hold still.'

I can't hold still, not while she's doing that to my nipples. She alternates – one in her mouth, the other between her fingers, leaving a trail of her saliva behind. My muscles clench with the effort to hold still, and I'm rewarded by the shifting of her body lower.

Her nails drag pleasantly along my sides until they reach my shorts. Her fingers grasp the band of them, and I lift my hips to help them off. She doesn't lower them, instead raising them up my body. The material of the seat digs into my sex, providing a hint of pressure against my clit. I feel the squelch it makes against my wet pussy, which throbs as she presses the material tight against me.

Then she's dragging it down and off my hips, exposing me to her. My thighs fall open in invitation, my hands roaming along my sides, grabbing my breasts and twirling my nipples. I want to see her face; I want to see what she thinks of me. I'm not self-conscious, not with Melody. She's been more accepting of me in our short time together than anyone else in my life.

I want to watch her marvel over me.

Her tongue is the first thing I feel, sliding along my right inner thigh. It stops just before my center, retreating to taste my other thigh the same way. I groan as she stops short, trying to spread my legs wider for her. Anything to direct her to my aching pussy.

She traces a finger from my hooded clit down to my

opening, dipping a finger inside of me. She withdraws it and there's a pause before the finger returns to wet my clit. It slides, slippery and waiting, under her fingers. My hips buck into her hand, wanting more – faster, harder, deeper.

Melody is as impatient as me. Her other hand dips between my legs, one finger sliding in and out of me in slow, steady pumps. Another finger joins the first, filling me. I'm so wet from her kisses and slow worship of my nipples. The headphones, the blindfold – they help. Not once have I thought of anything but where her hands and mouth are.

Oh, her mouth – there it is. Her lips curl over my clit and suck it into her mouth, her bottom teeth raking gently over the surface. I fail to stop my strangled cry – fuck my roommates. Like they've never brought someone over and fucked them.

Melody does it again, slower this time, her lips lingering over my sensitive bud. The feeling is too much and not enough, I need more. She slips a third finger inside of me, picking up her pace. Her tongue swirls over my clit, the sucking replaced with flicks and bites.

I'm so close.

I can't keep my hips still; they rock and buck against her face. My inner muscles clench on her fingers, trying to drag them deeper inside me. She keeps pace, her mouth making expert movements over my clit.

When I cum I'm seeing stars.

The build-up is quick – no languid rise, no gentle pressure, just the sudden onslaught of my orgasm. My back arches off the bed as I cum, my toes curling. Melody doesn't stop her thrusting fingers, but her tongue stills, trading the steady flicks for languid strokes. She pushes me through the orgasm, riding it out well past any orgasm I'd ever had before.

I whimper as Melody's fingers leave my soaked pussy. I reach for her, about to grab the blindfold and throw it to the side when her weight settles over my face. I grip her thighs on either side of my head, pulling her down over my face.

My tongue darts out for my first taste of her, rewarded with her saltwater taste. My tongue parts her lips, her wetness hitting my tongue right away. She's soaked already, the wetness from her thighs trailing along the side of my face.

I thrust my tongue into her opening and her hips drop to meet me. It's an awkward angle, but with some twisting of my shoulder, I bring my hand near my face, fingers tracing along the edges of her. I spread her lips with them, I trace from her clit to her open, waiting hole. I feel every angle of her with my tongue and fingers, wanting to memorize every inch of her.

She grinds on my face – wonton, needy, impatient.

I don't need an invitation.

I start with two fingers, easily sliding into her tight, wet hole. My tongue drags along her clit, sucking it into my mouth and letting it go with a pop. My fingers curl inside her, pressing against the soft inner padding of her walls. I hear her cry through my headphones, and I do it again, and again. She pushes herself onto my mouth, her fingers gripping my hair at the roots. I want her to tear it out, I want her to lose her mind on my mouth.

Two more quick thrusts and she's coming, her thighs tight along the side of my face. I flick her clit a few more times as she shivers on me, jumping at the sensation on her overstimulated clit.

She pushes the blindfold and headphones off, and I'm rewarded with her face. It's wet from my cum, glistening in the morning light. Her lips part as she pants, her brown eyes filled with barely sated lust as she stares down at me.

I've never seen anything so beautiful in my life.

10

———

MELODY

We are in bed all morning, and I can't think of anywhere else I'd rather be.

Yes, I suppose – looking for my skin, but that can wait a few hours, can't it? We'd explored most of the pier and the township attached to it.

I watch Addison sleep – humans sleep so much, and Addison is no exception. She slept all through the night after her nightmare, and now she's dozing again, her mouth partially open. She is peaceful like this, and I wonder if she ever knows peace when she's awake. I can see her thoughts warring with each other on her face as she tries to focus in a world that is much too loud for her.

She'd do better as a selkie than a human, where she could dive below the water and tune out the endless chatter of her world.

She stirs at last, stretching her bones and listening to them crack and pop. I mimic her, though mine don't make the same satisfying noise. Another difference between us despite how human I look without my skin.

"You hungry?" she asks. Her stomach growls a moment later and she gives a sheepish smile. I nod, and we dress and are off to the beach once more.

ADDISON IS quiet as we walk through the streets around her home to the breakfast place. I like this way of eating – 3 meals a day, sometimes a snack, all at reliable times. Hunting and getting fish whenever it's available is taxing, especially depending on where your pod lives. Mine picked a place close enough to the human fishing ground that we sometimes go hungry for a few days before a good meal can be found.

Humans, though – they have stores. Restaurants. Cafes.

Addison is only quiet when she's sleeping or thinking, and this worries me. Is she thinking that I've spent two nights with her and that's the extent of her hospitality? Is she thinking that if I hadn't kissed her first, she never would have kissed me?

Does she regret what we did in bed this morning? I

hope not – I very much want to do it again. And again. And again.

Worrying is not something I'm accustomed to. It must be the distance from my skin – it's getting to me. I've never been on land so long. My grandmother once told me that being separated from our skin for too long will cause melancholy, and that some selkies who are unable to get their skin back end up taking their lives.

"Are you a pescatarian?" Addison asks.

"A what?" I ask. I've already corrected her a few times about being a selkie. I thought she'd come to terms with it.

"A pescatarian. The only animal product they eat is fish," she says.

"I've never tried anything else," I admit.

"Really? You've never had a burger? A steak?" she presses.

"No, I really only eat raw fish, though I have gotten a squid once or twice before. Krill are fine, I prefer fish and mollusks though," I say. We've approached her breakfast spot, which smells like the pier on a hot day. The smells are nauseating when mixed in the humid air, and my stomach churns.

"Krill? How do you eat krill?" she asks, opening the door to the restaurant and stepping inside. Here the smells are worse, threatening to upturn my stomach. It's not empty yet after last night's meal.

"With my mouth," I say, swallowing hard.

Addison pauses and watches me, frowning. "Are you okay?"

"Um..." I start. I don't want to lie to her; this is her favorite breakfast place. She's gone through the trouble of taking me in, feeding me, and now she's sharing this with me. I cannot offend her when she's been so kind.

"Here, let's go outside," she says, resting her hand on my elbow. The sensation of her fingers against my human skin settles me, it's a balm to the pulsating illness roiling in my stomach. She guides me back out the door and into the cooler afternoon air. We settle at a table, her sitting next to me.

"Better?" she asks.

I nod, blushing. "I'm sorry, the smells..." I start.

She holds up her hand. "Hey, no, it's fine. I get overwhelmed sometimes too when it's loud or bright or there are too many people. Smells would do that, too, I guess."

"But this is your favorite spot," I say.

"Yeah, but I'm flexible. C'mon – all we've done is eat out, let me spoil you."

Spoil me.

Spoil is to rot. Spoil is to decay and die.

Addison means to...decay me?

I puzzle over the words as we walk through the

grocery store. I put a few things in my mouth to try them, which is against the rules.

"Oh, shit! Melody, we have to pay first," she says. My cheeks redden. She's not reprimanding me, not really – but I've once again misstepped in this human world.

The longing for my skin returns, my body raw and exposed without it. I stop in front of a case of fish, my heart stuttering. Never in my life have I seen them all laid out like this – already killed, stripped, waiting to be eaten. I salivate as I press my fingers against the glass. If only my family could see this!

"Whatcha want?" asks the man behind the counter.

"That," I say, pointing to the delicious white fish with its head still attached.

"Bag it up," Addison says with a shrug. I rock on my toes as he allows me to pick exactly which fish I want, even allowing me to smell them before I make my deci-sion. Addison smiles as we walk through the store, adding items to her cart. She lets me pick things, asking if I like sauces or spices. I politely decline – the fish is enough.

The smell taunts me from the bags the entire way home.

"Sit," she says, pointing to a chair in her cooking room. I've learned each room has a purpose – this one is where she prepares food, the other is where you sit, and the last is where you sleep and make love.

"Is that fish?" comes a voice from the sitting room. A man stands there, his eyes heavy-lidded with sleep, his brow furrowed.

"Oh, hey, Emilio," Addison says, her gaze darting from him to me. "Yeah, I was just making us some brunch."

"Of fish?" he says. His gaze turns to me, giving me a once-over. "Is this who's been spending the night?"

"Hello, I'm Melody," I say.

"Emilio," he replies, not moving any deeper into the cooking room.

"Yeah, she's in town for a bit, needed a place to stay," Addison says.

I try to hide my conspiratorial smile – she is keeping my secret from the man who lives with her. They may share a home, but he is not close enough to be privy to this information.

"Whatever – just clean up after, okay?" he says, slinking back into his rooms.

"Sorry about him – he's picky about smells. And messes. And being paid on time," Addison says with a shrug. She unloads the food we got from the store, and I crane my neck to watch what she does with the fish.

"So – raw fish. Do you have to like...do anything to it? To make sure it doesn't have disease on it?" she asks.

"I never do," I say with a tilt of my head. Disease? Like what?

"Okay – and the seaweed?" she asks, pulling out a bag of it.

My eyes widen – an entire *bag* of seaweed, ready for the eating! "It's fine as it is," I say, squirming in my chair.

She turns the bag over to read the back, frowning. "The preparation directions are in another language... if you're sure, I guess."

I nod enthusiastically.

"So you just...eat all of this, raw? Just slap it on the plate and you're good to go?" she presses. I nod again.

"Wow, easy date. Okay..." She fumbles in the cabinets and takes out a plate, which she loads with the fish and the seaweed. "Bon appetit, I guess?"

She doesn't have to tell me twice – I dig into the food with relish. The fish is a little old, not as fresh as if I'd caught it myself, but it's larger than most of the fish I've found lately. I groan as I take the first bite, scooping up a mass of seaweed on a fork. It takes a lot of restraint not to just pick it up with my hands. Humans disapprove of this method. Addison watches me with rapt attention, her gaze darting from my lips to my hands.

"Oh, sorry – did you want some?" I ask, extending a forkful of the seaweed.

"No, thanks...it looks..." She trails off. "It's not for me, I guess. Maybe at a restaurant some time. You're sure you're not going to get some disease from it being uncooked?"

"Uh-uh," I say, taking another big bite. I've heard of disease, I've seen my family get sick from old age or something they picked up on the shore. From food? Never.

"Thank you," I say, pausing between bites of the fish.

"Hmm?" she asks. She has that faraway look in her eyes, like she can see through every wall in the house and onto the street.

"For this," I say. "For spoiling me."

"Oh, it's nothing – you have to eat, after all," she says.

"Yes, but you've fed me. Clothed me. Given me a place to sleep, helped me find my skin," I tell her. My chest is too full of these feelings, my head too full of these thoughts – she needs to hear them.

Her gaze is fire on my skin, leaving prickling heat wherever she looks. Right now, she's focused on my mouth, and I flick my tongue out to taste if some fish is clinging to my lip. She sucks in a breath, her eyes widening a fraction.

I imagine what it would be like to lick seaweed and fish from Addison's skin. Unfortunately, I've eaten all of it. I swallow the last bit, lost in Addison's gaze. Her eyes narrow, puzzling through something.

"Tell me," I breathe. I don't know why my voice is so quiet.

"I was just thinking..." She starts, then shakes her head. "I'd rather show you."

"Show me?" I echo, tilting my head in thought.

She stands slowly, her lips pulling into a devious smile. I stand as well, hand reaching out to touch her. My hands feel empty without some part of her in them. She doesn't shy away from my touches. She steps into them, filling me with more of her. She kisses my jaw and I whimper, wanting more.

I follow her to her room. I'd follow her anywhere.

I don't wait for her prompting, I pull my borrowed top and shorts off. Her gaze is hot on my skin, tracing from my toes to the top of my head.

"I was wondering," she says, using her body to push me back onto the bed. I drop on it, crawling backward on my elbows. "If you've ever used a vibrator."

"A what?" I ask, blinking. I don't recognize the word and it feels out of place in this conversation.

The look on her face is unmistakable – she wants this. She wants me. I open my mouth to ask her to explain when she opens a drawer in her dresser and removes a small item. It looks like a short, wider writing utensil. She strips and crawls across the bed to hover over me.

Her kiss is all heat and passion, sending a shock down to my toes. I arch into her, trying to pull her on top of me, wanting every exposed bit of my skin covered with her own. Her hand slides between my legs and I hear a click, then...

OH. Oh.

The sensation is unlike anything I've felt in my life. The buzzing on my pussy vibrates across my entire body. She traces the vibrator from between my lips to my clit and my vision swims. I have to shut my eyes tight to keep my senses. The buzz is gentle, but insistent, sending thrills along my aching body. My fingers tighten on the sheets under me, doing anything to ground me. My body wants to give in, to crest to the top of an orgasm but I have to resist. Once I come the vibrations will stop, and I cannot have that.

There's another click and the vibrations stop.

My eyes fly open, gazing up at Addison's worried face.

"Is it...does it hurt? I'm so sorry, I just..." she starts, pulling the item away.

I grab her arm before she can retreat from me. "Please," I beg. I can't finish the sentence; I can't form a thought. I want that vibrator on me again.

Addison sucks in a breath, her eyes widening. Another click, and then it's back, pressed gently against my wetness. I'm dripping now, I can feel it track down my body to the bed below.

This time she is softer, gentler as she presses onto my heated flesh. I grind against her hand, wanting for the full force of it. I want her hesitance to evaporate, I want her to use this item to consume me.

Addison kisses my cheek, then my collarbone, then my breast. She rolls my nipple around her mouth, her teeth making soft impressions on the skin. She slips a finger into me and moves the vibrator up my pussy, gently pressing on my clit. Her lips circle my nipple, sucking gently then letting go with a loud *pop*. She does the same to the other, coaxing them to a firm peak, driving me closer and closer to orgasm.

Her mouth, the vibrator, her fingers inside me – it's all too much.

The first wave of my orgasm tracks up my body from my core to my mouth. I tilt my head back, unable to suppress the gasping cry as I cum. My heels dig into the bed as I rock against Addison's hand, my fingers tightening in the sheets under me. Addison is with me through it all, rocking the vibrator along my spasming pussy, pushing me from one wave to another. I crest one just to crash into another, the muscles in my body clenching then relaxing, an endless cycle of pleasure dragged out until I am too sensitive to touch.

Addison eases away from my hot sex, gathering me into her arms as I fall asleep with her.

11

ADDISON

I already hated working but working while knowing that a beautiful woman waited for me at home is near torture. That morning, she clung to me like I was a lifeline when I crawled out of bed at the last minute. I couldn't be late for work; I was too new for that shit. I thought about calling in sick and curling back into bed with Melody but...again, too new for that shit.

Melody's pout as I left her alone in my room pulled at my heartstrings. At least there was food in the fridge so she'd have something to eat and wouldn't have to wander the streets alone. According to her, she'd been doing that for years. The thought concerned me, especially since she had no money, identification, or wallet.

Sitting in Monday evening traffic was another type of cruel and unusual punishment. It was likely in the Geneva Convention – commuting to an office, where you spent half of the day on conference calls, only to commute hours home. Public transit who? Not in gas-guzzling America.

After what felt like a decade, I park in front of the house and practically skip to the door. My hand hovers before the knob, panicked. What if she left? What if she was really a crazy person who stole everything we owned? Well, joke's on her, we have nothing to steal.

I realize then I'm more worried that she's gone than her possible kleptomania. Only one way to find out – insert the key into the knob, turn the door, and peer through the dark house. Emilio's car is gone, as is Holly's bike and Tally's moped. I'm the first one home.

"Melody?" I call into the darkness. All the shades are pulled, and all the lights are off. It takes a moment for my eyes to adjust to the figure that peers around the corner of the hall to my room. She wears one of my t-shirts, which is much too large on her, and likely nothing else. I'm glad I'd made a stop at lunch to grab her more clothes.

"Addison!" she greets brightly.

"Hope you weren't too bored today," I offer with an awkward laugh.

She shakes her head, crossing the room to wrap her arms around me in a hug. I melt into it, unable to suppress the sigh that slips past my lips. "I did miss you," she says into my shoulder. When she pulls away,

I feel empty. I've never had a hug like that before, much less had anyone excited for me to get home.

"Well, I brought you some clothes. Not that I don't like how you look wearing mine, but..." I hold out the bag in my hand.

"For me?" she asks, reaching out tentatively to take the bag from me.

"Yeah, it's nothing really. There's a place near my office, where I get my lunch. I just saw something that reminded me of you, it's not a big deal. Plus, you don't have clothes, you know? I figured you couldn't go look today, and you were probably sick of wearing the same thing..."

I trail off as she pulls the shorts and tank top from the bag, her mouth making an 'O' as she turns them over in her hands. She pulls my shirt off and flings it onto the ground, exposing her naked body. I suck in a breath, my gaze roving over her flesh. She slips the shorts on then the tank top, running her hands along the fabric. "It's so soft," she says. The cold air pebbles her nipples, making them visible through the thin fabric.

"I would have gotten you underwear or a bra, but I wasn't sure what size you were. We can...we can go grab some now?" I suggest. It takes every ounce of discipline to drag my attention back to her face.

Melody's smirk is knowing, but she nods and

extends her hand to take mine. "I will go with you wherever you'd like," she says.

"Let me change first," I say, hurrying to my bedroom. She follows, her gaze tracking me as I strip quickly and replace my business slacks and blouse for a pair of shorts and a t-shirt. I slip on a pair of sandals and nod to the door.

"You hungry?" I ask.

She shakes her head. "Not yet, but I will be."

"Good. I know just the place."

12

MELODY

I thought Addison would never return.

I tried my best to get her to stay but Addison was not easily swayed. She stood in the doorway to her bedroom before she left for work, her mouth a thin line. I think I pushed too hard, but I wanted her to stay. I wanted to cuddle up to her all day and walk the beach with her all afternoon. I wanted to eat fish and have her spoil me.

But I am an adult, so I busy myself. I walk the neighborhood, I look for my skin in a few less obvious places. I borrow some food from a corner market, shoving it into my mouth before anyone notices it's missing.

I used to be able to lose myself for hours on this boardwalk alone. The stores, the food, the people – it's such a treat. I find myself turning to point something out to Addison, only to remember she's at work. At an office. Perhaps that is the fate my ancestors warned us about – destined to be locked in a room with no windows and no doors. The way Addison describes her work it sounds much the same.

The morning dips to the afternoon, so I take a nap on the sand. An Angry Man tries to chase me away, saying I can't loiter on the beach. I don't know what he's talking about – I don't have any trash; I dispose of it all in the overflowing cans along the roadway. I've seen what it does in my home the ocean, of the islands of trash that float far offshore. I try to tell him this, he just insists that I can't loiter.

My nap has been interrupted, my mood soured, so I return to Addison's home. My temporary home.

Addison is still gone, so I put on one of her t-shirts until she returns. I bring the hem to my nose and inhale her scent, loving the material against my bare human skin. When her voice echoes through the hallway I have to contain my excitement and walk casually out to greet her.

This is what I wanted earlier – hand in hand, walking through the streets. She helps me buy some clothing to wear under my clothing, which feels silly until I see the way she looks at me as I tried them on. She looks like a shark waiting for its chance to strike.

We walk along the sidewalk that borders the beach and Addison tells me about her day and what she did at work. I don't understand any of it, but I nod along. It's better than explaining that selkies don't really have *jobs*. We have duties that we perform to support our family, but that isn't the same as leaving home to go to an office all day.

Yeck. Boring. Awful.

"Want to go on the beach?" I ask. If I don't dip my toes into the water, I think I might shrivel up and blow away. Addison nods, and we make our way to the shore. I kick off my shoes and skip through the sand until my feet hit the water and let out a happy sigh.

"I missed this," I tell her.

"The beach?" she asks. "We were here like... yesterday."

"No, the water," I say, nodding to the break. "I've never gone this long without my skin, without swimming in the water."

"You must be a strong swimmer," Addison says.

"Selkies generally are. In our seal form, we have fins and a tail that help us. The current is nothing for us," I reply proudly. I'm an especially strong swimmer, and very fast. I'd love to show Addison one day if I ever find my skin again. The thought saddens me, so I keep it to myself.

"And you're not scared?" Addison asks, incredulous.

"Scared? Of what?"

"Oh, man, what isn't there to be scared of? First of

all, there's the rip tides, they can pull you under and really far out. I see signs about them all the time. Then there's the algae, I've heard there's been some awful blooms lately, of this like toxic algae that's making some of the animals go crazy. Plus there's sharks. Haven't you seen the movie about the surfer who gets her arm bit off by a shark? You have vital arteries and shit in your arm, you can bleed to death like *that*." She snaps to accentuate her point.

I open my mouth to protest but she continues. "And say you don't deal with the sharks or the algae or whatever...there's all sorts of wild fish. I once watched a documentary of a woman who had a swordfish impale her chest and pushed part of her breast implant into her lungs. No doctor could figure it out and she just suffered for like, months." She shudders and wraps her arms around herself.

I wrap my arms around her. "What if," I say, "you go into the water and it's beautiful? And you swim and jump and play in the waves?"

"Or step on a sea urchin and need emergency surgery," she counters.

"Then step where I do," I say, dragging her deeper into the water. She resists, her heels digging into the shore. "Just a few steps," I plead. She relents, chewing on her lip as she takes a few steps into the water. It's up to our knees now, but I need more. Luckily a wave hits us and splashes us, soaking us to our shoulders.

"Oh god!" Addison says, crying out in surprise.

"Guess we gotta go all the way in now," I say, jumping into the next wave. I let it carry me back to the beach, screaming in joy all the while. Addison watches with wild eyes, clutching her chest as I stand and jog back into the water to her side.

"Holy shit, I thought you'd fallen and cracked your head or something!" she says.

"Here comes another – c'mon!" I cry, jumping into it. Addison watches, shifting her weight. When I return to her side a second time, I note the goosebumps along her arm. "One..." I count, watching the wave roll in. I grab her hands in my own and smile at her. "Two..." I say, leaning forward to press my lips to hers. "Three!"

She jumps with me, and we're caught up in the wave, toppling back to shore in a mess of limbs. When I turn to her, she's laughing, standing to run into the water again. I follow her and we throw ourselves into the waves time and time again, until we're both so exhausted that we let the wave wash us up on the shore.

"That was fun," Addison says, collapsing onto the sand just beyond the water's edge. "Thank you."

"For what?" I ask, sitting next to her. We're close enough for our bodies to touch, and I lean against her and rest my head on her shoulder. The sun is starting to sink behind the horizon, sending long shadows along the mostly empty portion of the beach.

"I...I get into my head a lot," she admits. "It makes it hard to be in the moment and just enjoy stuff. How... how do you do it?"

"Do what?" I ask.

"Just...enjoy things. Not immediately think of the worst thing that could happen?"

I shift to turn to look at her. She avoids my eyes, training them instead on the ocean water. Her bottom lip is caught between her teeth, and I want to kiss it out of her worrying mouth. "Welllllll," I say. "I guess I just...don't worry about what I can't control? I can't control the sharks or the waves or the sea urchins, so I don't try. Will worrying about the shark keep it from biting you?"

"No, but if you worry about the shark so you don't get into the water then you won't get bitten," she says. She chances a glance at me, then back away to the water.

"But then you'd never get in the water. If you don't try, you're always left wondering."

"Better to love and have lost than never love at all," she says.

"What?" I ask, my heart fluttering at the sound of 'love' from her mouth. I don't love Addison, that is silly, but hearing her say the word makes my stomach tumble. One day I'd like to hear her say that word.

"Oh, it's a saying," she says quickly, clamping her jaw shut. Her eyes become unfocused and she's going into her mind again, far away from me. I jealously want her here with me. I suppose it's okay to be selfish during times like that.

"Tell me," I press, nudging her arm. She jerks to attention, blinking at me. "Huh?"

"Tell me what you were thinking, where you went." It's a demand now, and I try to make my face stern.

Her lips quirk in a smile and she shakes her head. "It's okay," she says.

"No, it's not okay – I want to know."

"Fine. It's a phrase, a saying – better to love and have lost than never love at all. I think I heard it in school, and I started to think of what class I would have heard it in. Maybe English class, since I'm sure someone old and stuffy wrote it. I tried to think of other phrases we had to learn from old poets, and I realized I couldn't think of any of their names, except Shakespeare. Then I remembered that most of the movies I watched when I was a kid were reimaginations of his plays, kind of like fanfic...and then you asked what I was thinking."

"Wow," I say.

"Yeah, that's what my mind is like. Don't take it personally if I kinda...zone out," she says.

"Can you...can you take me with next time?" I ask.

Her eyebrows shoot up her face. "You're serious? That doesn't like...bother you? That we'd be talking about something and I'm thinking of something else?"

"Only if you don't share it with me," I offer. "There's so many interesting things about your life and this world. I want to know them all. I want to know all of you."

"I'm pretty boring," Addison says, squirming. She doesn't try to move away from me, but I can feel her muscles tense against my body.

I lean forward to place a kiss on her shoulder. "That's okay. All I did all day was swim around and eat. The only school I know is...fish."

Addison laughs at that, and my heart expands. The wrinkle between her brow flattens and she bumps my shoulder with her own. "Okay, I'll take you on my mind journeys...if you promise to make me do things that scare me. Not all the time...maybe once a day?"

"Okay," I say. She extends her hand, and I grab it in my own, surprised when she moves her arm up and down quickly.

"Deal," she says.

"Deal," I repeat.

13

ADDISON

The end of the day can't come fast enough.

I met Melody exactly seven days ago and it feels like forever and no time at all.

Every evening, I get home from work, and we begin our 'search' anew – sifting through the thrift stores along the inner portions of the boardwalk or asking the lifeguards that dot the shore. Most of them frown and shake their head. Every 'no' slows Melody's step a bit more, every empty bin at the thrift store is another nail in the coffin.

Her skin – whatever that looks like or means – is gone.

I can't help but wonder what that means for *us*. She shows no signs of leaving, she makes no inquiries about hotels or apartments where she can stay in the area. Every night she curls up into bed with me, and every day I return from work she's ready to head out again.

Does she even have money? A job? I'm afraid to ask, her answers are always more cryptic than helpful.

Traffic on Thursday afternoon heading to the beach makes me want to pry my eyes out with a screwdriver. It's been twenty minutes, and I don't think I've gone more than two or three miles. The sound of my grinding brakes sets my teeth on edge and I'm forced to keep a good distance between the car in front of me and myself. One bump and my junker would be totaled.

Hell, pigeon shit would total my car, for all it's worth.

I watch a man pushing a shopping cart slowly come into focus as I start/stop my way along the interstate. Normally it'd be dangerous for a pedestrian to walk on the side of the road like this, but none of us are going more than ten miles an hour at a time. He's probably safer walking here than on the streets.

Maybe that's where Melody lived before I met her? I tossed her filthy clothes the minute I bought her something else to wear. She didn't act particularly upset by their loss. She would have told me, right?

Maybe. Every discussion about her life is shrouded in that strange story about the selkies. It's probably a trauma response – I should ask my therapist at our next appointment.

Oh, shit. I missed it – it was on Wednesday.

The man is closer now, just a few car lengths ahead of me. His cart has a wheel that spins in circles, further cementing how slowly we're moving. I hit the steering wheel a few times, cursing the fact that I wanted to move to California.

Not only California – *the beach*. No money, no skill or talent, no reason to live where I do. It meant I was forever doomed to drive a shit car and live with roommates because the likelihood of me affording my own place was zero.

The man with the cart pauses, leaning against the cement barrier. He shades his eyes as he surveys the interstate. Sweat coats the front and back of his shirt and his hair is plastered to his forehead. I glance in the rearview mirror at the slope behind me. Damn, the guy was pushing that shopping cart *uphill*. No wonder he's spent.

Something in the cart catches my eye. It looks like a wet suit, but it's a slate-gray color. It's shoved near the bottom of his cart, folded to fit. The fins, which resemble a tail, flop over the side of the cart. The sun catches the edge of the cart and blinds me for a moment. I blink away the black spots on my vision, the cart little more than a shadow against the backdrop.

I'm nearly level with the man now. I lean across the passenger seat to grab the window crank, lowering the passenger window. It sticks for a moment, then lowers all the way.

"Hey!" I shout to the man.

He jogs a few feet to my car, ducking his head into the window. "What?" he asks. He stops short at the sight of me, clearly not who he was expecting.

"What's that?" I ask, pointing to his cart.

"My shit, what's it to you?" he asks. He's taken a step back now, his brows furrowing.

"No, the gray thing. The fin," I said, waving at the cart.

He tosses a quick look over his shoulder, his frown deepening. "I found it, I didn't steal it," he says.

"Didn't say you did. Just curious what it is," I say.

"I didn't kill it, either," he adds.

"Didn't say that," I grind out. Traffic starts to move again, so if he doesn't wrap this up, I'll lose him forever. There's no way in hell I could turn around.

"Yeah, well, I didn't," he presses.

"I think it belongs to my friend," I tell him.

"You don't even know what it is, but it belongs to your friend?" he asks.

The car behind me honks and I flip them off. He can go around me for all I give a shit, if he can squeeze.

"It's a wet suit, a full one," I try. It's the best I can approximate to what Melody described. *Looks like skin, me sized, selkies are seals.* What the hell else was I supposed to think?

"Huh," the man says, crossing his arms over his chest.

"Yeah, so – I'd like to give it back to her," I say.

The man laughs and shakes his head. "Nice try, but it's mine."

"You said you found it, which means someone else lost it," I press. Now the entire line of cars behind me is honking, loud enough that I can't make out his response.

"Look, I'll give you cash for it. How about $50?" I ask.

"It's a pretty nice wet suit," the man says with a smile.

"$60 then," I say. I throw the bird again to the line of cars behind me, which just makes them honk louder.

Fuckers, can't they see I'm negotiating?

"$80," the man says.

"Done," I say, putting my car into park. I cross in front of my car to his cart, helping him to extract the items from it. It's flattened in some areas, with creases along the middle of it from where it's been folded. I toss him a wad of cash and open my trunk to throw it in. I pause, considering the full sight of it. It looks exactly like the skin of a seal and feels like I imagine they feel - rubbery, soft. The tail and fins are in all the right places, the face distorted and flat without anything to fill it.

Another honk pulls me from my reverie. I slam the trunk and give the guy behind me the double bird and consider grabbing my nonexistent junk. Nah – I gotta get home.

I climb into the driver's seat and take the car out of park, moving the four car lengths the cars progressed in the last few minutes. The honking stops, we're at a standstill again.

Melody is going to *freak* when I tell her! Her skin – found at last – and on the *interstate* of all places. We'll have a great laugh about it, and then maybe she'll show me how she puts the damn thing on. The logistics of blow my mind – does she keep her legs together, and put a foot in each flipper of the tail? Does she curl her arms up to put them in the side fins?

How does she swim in it? How does she *breathe* in it?

I'll have to take a better look, or she can explain it to me before she leaves.

I flinch at the thought. *Before she leaves*. This is the only reason she's stuck around. If we'd found her skin on day one, she'd be gone – back to her family, who surely misses her. Back to wherever she came from.

She has no job here; she hasn't asked how to find an apartment or a place to live. *She has no intention of staying, that's why*. Once she found this hunk of weird rubbery stuff, she fully planned to pack up her meager belongings and bounce. When I found her, she didn't even have a toothbrush! Or a change of clothes! That is not someone who plans on staying!

I'm such an idiot. I'd spent this whole last week going about my day, not even aware that she could be *gone* when I got home. Would she even leave a letter? Or would she disappear, another person slipping through my fingers?

Unless...

No.

I couldn't. I can't. It would be so fucked up if I just... got rid of it. Destroyed it, hid it – whatever. It'd mean she'd stay...but for how much longer? How long until her infatuation with me fades? When she realizes the skin is gone forever, and she doesn't need to stick around with a burn out like me.

It would only be a matter of time. She'd want something more from her life and I wouldn't be able to give it to her. She'd move on and I'd stay here, in my small house near the ocean, with nothing to offer her.

It's only been a week; you can't really get to know someone in a week. Maybe with some more time, another week or two, she'd realize that we have something special. I've never felt this way before, in a friendship or relationship.

She hasn't had a chance to realize what this was, or what this could be. With another week or two, I could improve. I could do more at work, maybe ask after a promotion. Fuck, I hadn't cleaned my room since we met – I'd do that when I got home. Show her that I wasn't a complete slob.

Another week – maybe two – and she'd see what I could offer. I just needed to be better, be less Addison and more...Addison 2.0. New, improved, wanting to impress the beautiful woman she met on the beach a week ago.

Two weeks. Maybe three.

A month, possibly.

How long does it take for someone to fall in love? Whoa, pump the brakes – love is a big word. Love is a... fuck, these idiots honking behind me need to chill out. We're moving at the speed of smell, just because I didn't inch forward the moment the car in front of me did doesn't mean we're going to get cut off.

It's decided – I'll keep the skin in my trunk for a few weeks-ish. Just enough time to improve some things in Addison land, get Melody to see what I have to offer. Then I'll tell her I found the skin somewhere and I'll be the good guy for once. She won't want to leave because she'll see how great this thing we have is.

Yeah. Just a few months, nothing more than that.

That night, we lay in bed and talk and laugh. The skin is like that story I read in high school – the guy that kills that person and puts them into a wall? And he can hear their heart beating until it drives him mad? I always thought it was a stupid story. You got away with murder! No one will find out! You won!

Instead, the thought of the skin shoved into my trunk, bouncing around with old energy drink cans and dirt and hair pounds through my head. When I close my eyes, I see her tear-stained face under that dock the first night I met her. The next morning, I wake early and stare at my car from the window, hoping someone stole it. If it's gone then it's out of my hands – not my fault. I tried! Sorry! The old beast is still parked on the street.

I need something to distract me from this. I grab my phone and text my only friends.

14

MELODY

Addison has a surprise.

I'm not sure what that means, because everything here is a surprise. The cat that purrs in my lap, the taste of the food she has in her kitchen, her human skin against mine. Everything is new and bright and beautiful.

Addison is not good at secrets. She tells me what I need to bring – a bathing suit (I procure one while she's busy), a dress, sandals. She's in the kitchen packing food together, including an assortment of fish she bought for me. Addison is thoughtful like that – after I was sickened by the smell of her food, we avoided indoor eating establishments. She says it's too beautiful to be inside.

If my family could see me now! If they could get to know Addison, the way she is so kind and tender even as her mind flails in the waves, they would know that not all humans are bad. Our ancestors simply found the wrong ones.

Now we can find *them* and pick them ourselves.

Addison hops into her car and leans over to open the door to my side. I've not yet experienced the inside of the car, but I know that if you cross in front of them you need to make sure they're not moving. They're like boats, but the danger is at the front and not the back.

"C'mon," she says, leaning across the seat to look up at me. Her red hair falls across her forehead, and I slip into the seat, reaching out to push it behind her ear. Her lips twitch in a smile and I like the sight of that, so I kiss her.

Her kiss in return is full of heat – lips pressed against mine, full of wanting and warmth.

But she breaks the kiss to settle into her seat. She reaches up to a strap that hangs, securing it around her body with a click. I mimic her, not liking the feel of the material against my body. It feels too much like a net. I push against it, but it doesn't give. It clicks into place, pinning me against the seat.

"Here," Addison says. She pulls on the strap and slips it behind my body. "If we get pulled over by a cop put it back. I'm not in the mood to get another ticket."

I relax into the seat, no longer held immobile.

That is, until the car starts to *move*. If being outside the car is scary, being inside of it is infinitely worse. It lurches, almost sending me from my seat. Addison scoffs. "I'm not that bad of a driver!"

My fingers dig into the cushion as she maneuvers the car impossibly through the streets, stopping and going with no rhyme or reason. Eventually, we are no longer stopping and starting, but cruising at a steady pace alongside other cars. I like this.

I like it even more when Addison reaches down to ratchet a knob on her door and the wind from outside pours into the car. I laugh and mimic her movements, allowing the wind in on my side as well. My hair blows in my face, obscuring my vision, but I don't care. It reminds me of home, of the way the waves pull and tug at my hair when I shed my skin.

My skin. I'm reminded of its loss again and it aches.

But I won't let it dull the moment. Addison has been at work all week, and I missed her. The nights spent curled up to her are too short, despite their sweetness. It's a balance between allowing her enough sleep so she is not grumpy the next day and filling every moment together with laughter and love.

Love. The word tickles, but I don't shy away from it.

I relax into the seat and let the wind blow over my face until Addison slows the car. I smell the ocean break through the noxious fumes of the car.

I know this beach – it is one I've seen only from the water, not daring to walk on its shore. There is no boardwalk, no pier to hide under, just miles and miles of fluffy sand and people. Addison cruises around until she finds a spot to leave the car. Her gaze wavers to the back portion of her car and she opens her mouth to say something. Then she shakes her head and turns toward the beach. We walk, hand in hand, to the sand.

"Addy! Over here!"

Addison turns her head to a small group of humans that settle in the sand. She waves and tugs me along until we are standing over them. "Hey guys," she says shyly. The group gazes from our joined hands to my face, and I smile at them.

"Who's your friend?" asks one of the women. She's tall and lanky, spread out on the ground on a towel. Her tan skin glistens with sweat under the sun, her dark black hair braided down her back. She wears sunglasses, which she lowers to get a better look at me.

"This is Melody," Addison says. Her hand is warm and sweaty in mine. I step toward her, increasing the contact with our bodies. Comforting.

"Melody," Addison says again. "This is Samira," she nods to the woman with the glasses.

"Natalie," she points to a pale, freckled woman who sits under an umbrella, her face hidden under a large-brimmed hat.

"Stefan," a man lounging near Natalie, his olive-toned skin covered in tattoos that snake up his arms and along his chest.

"And Brig," nodding to another woman wearing a

wet suit, with wisps of blonde hair that cling to her face.

"Hello," I say, repeating their names to myself as I follow their faces. It's not easy to tell humans apart, placing names with them should help.

"Pop a squat," Stefan says, patting the sand next to him. Addison keeps her hand in mine and leads me to the sand next to him.

"So...Melody, where you from?" asks Natalie.

"The ocean," I say. These are Addison's friends, surely I can be as honest with them as I have been with her.

"The ocean?" Stefan says, sitting upright. "Like... Ocean Beach? Oceanside? Baja?"

"Everywhere," I tell him, unfamiliar with the names.

"Ah, army brat – I get it, we moved all the time when I was a kid," says Natalie. "Landed here last, never left."

"Melody Of the Ocean," Stefan says, and it sounds like a song. "How did you meet our dear friend Addison?" He wraps and arm around her as he says this, bringing her close to his side. She leans away from him, her muscles tense.

"She helped me look for something I lost," I say.

"Addison lending a helping hand to a stranger? No way," Brig says with a laugh.

"Wow Brig, right in the heart," Addison laughs, but

it's a different laugh than the one I'm used to. More guarded, quieter. I don't like it.

"She's been very helpful," I continue. "I've been staying with her, she feeds me, and she helps me look for it at night."

Samira pulls off her large sunglasses to stare openly at Addison. "Addison? As in, the Addison sitting next to you?"

I nod.

"Huh," Brig says, crossing her arms over her chest. "I never thought I'd see the day."

"Oh stop," Addison says, shaking her head. Her cheeks flush red and she's slouched into herself, shrinking on herself. I place my hand on her knee and smile at her. These are her friends; surely they are aware of her kindness? Her generosity?

"Is it so hard to believe?" I ask, my gaze moving from one person to another in the group.

"Yes!" They say in unison, then laugh. Addison laughs with them, the same quiet laugh she used before.

"Don't buy their fake superiority," Addison says once the laughter dies down. "Natalie's been with her boyfriend for years, despite him being a serial cheater. Samira had to start frequenting bars the next city over because of her reputation. Stefan only dates beautiful women that want nothing to do with him and Brig..." She points at each of them as she speaks, pausing on the blonde woman. Brig smiles, showing a row of perfectly white teeth.

"I am untamed," she says. "Wild and free – nothing to hold me down."

"Exactly – no boyfriend, no job, no nothing," Samira says, frowning at her.

Brig shrugs. "Listen, as much as I'd love to be part of the material world like all of you – I have more exciting things to do. Like," she says, grabbing a tall, flat item that lays discarded next to her in the sand, "catching this wave. Bye!" Brig jumps up and runs into the waves with it. I've seen humans on it before, swam under them as they tumbled among the waves on their long boards.

"Wow – what a read," Natalie says. "Of course, Addison leaves herself out of her assessment. Always late, forgetful, selfish, doesn't listen when people talk to her, can't hold down a job," Natalie ticks off on her fingers.

"C'mon, Nat, that's unfair. Addy, it was cruel to laugh at you. And Melody, you're in good hands with Addison. She's got a tough shell, but inside, she's all goo," Stefan says. "Plus, you're the first person she's ever brought around us."

"For this exact reason. C'mon, Melody – want to go for a swim?" Addison says.

I nod and we stand, discarding our shoes near the towels and stepping into the water.

"Jesus, I forgot how cold it is," Addison says once our toes touch the water. It is chilly without my skin, but it's refreshing after the heat of the sun. I take her hand, enjoying the feel of her palm against my own. She glances down at our joined hands, then up at my face.

"I'm sorry about my friends," she says. "I don't know why I thought it'd be different if I..." She trails off, shaking her head.

"Do you like them?" I ask.

She laughs. "Most of the time. Sometimes, though...it's different here than back home. People are a little crueler; it's like a personality trait. Move to a Cali beach, become a Cali cunt."

I don't understand the reference, but I nod anyway. The way she enunciates the word *cunt* makes me think it's a harsh word. Mean.

"You are not a cunt," I say.

She stills, her hand pulsing in mine. "I am, though," she says, looking to the horizon. The waves are far out, and some of the humans are swimming and riding their long flat boards. I can't pick out Brig, the reflection is too bright to tell.

"Do you like it here?" she asks.

"I prefer your room," I tell her honestly, moving closer to her.

She laughs and shakes her head. "No, I mean... here. Not with your family."

"It's…" I trail off. I can't describe it. Being with my family is all I know, it's where I grew up. It's all I've ever known. This place is scary, loud, bright – there's nowhere to hide. I do nothing all day except look for my skin. I am aimless, caught in a current I can't see and can't control.

"Oh," Addison says. She must read it on my face. "I assume when you get your skin, you'll go back?"

"I must," I tell her. I have to tell my family I'm okay, to let them know I wasn't captured or killed. Not knowing what happened to me will haunt them.

I step deeper into the water, letting it ebb and flow around my waist. Addison shivers in the water, and I pull her close, our bodies warming each other. She opens her mouth to speak a few times before shutting it closed. She sometimes brings me along with her when her mind wanders, but sometimes I think it wanders too far for her comfort. Like now, as she stares at the beach and chews on her lip. I want to ask her if she's thinking of the sharks, or maybe she's playing over the words of her friends, but instead I enjoy the feel of her body against mine.

The rest of the day is beautiful.

Addison's friends teach me how to play a game called volleyball. I am clumsy in the sand and on foot. Even a week as a human isn't enough time to learn all the intricacies of movement, and I fall many times. I laugh and try again, pleased that Addison's friends enjoy my company.

When the sun is high in the sky we sit and eat. Addison opens the box we brought and hands me the fish she's kept on ice. Her friends watch curiously.

"She's a pescatarian," Addison tells them. I want to correct her – *selkie* – but their teasing from before gives me pause. It's too soon to tell them, I must bide my time like I did with Addison.

Addison goes to grab something from the car, and I am left alone with Natalie and Brig.

"I've never seen her this happy," Brig says, nodding her head in Addison's direction.

"Yeah, she never comes to beach day," Natalie agrees.

"Really?" I ask. I don't understand why – we met on the beach. She lives near the beach. We spend most of our time wandering along the edges of it.

"Yeah, she's usually..." Brig trails off, reaching into the air as if she can pick the words from it.

"Addison can be a bitch," Natalie says.

I glare at her, making to stand. Natalie reaches out to grab my arm, dragging me down. "Look – you seem like a nice girl. Too nice for Addison. There's a reason she's never brought anyone around; it doesn't take long for the real Addison to come out."

I wrest my arm from her grip, glaring. "Addison has

been nothing but kind to me," I say. "She deserves better friends."

"Don't say I didn't warn you," Natalie says, standing to leave.

Brig watches her go, then levels her gaze on me. "Natalie calling Addison a bitch is a bit pot meet kettle," she says with a laugh.

I don't laugh with her – it sounds mean, whatever it means.

"I think what she meant to say," Brig says, leaning closer to me. "Is that Addison will dig a hole, and sometimes she drags others in with her. None of us are perfect, so we don't fault her for it. We do, however, move away when she pulls out the shovel. You get it?"

I don't, but I nod anyway. I want to leave; I want to go back to our home where we're safe from these cruel people who call themselves her *friends*. My friends would never say anything like this about me when I'm not around. How can they be so kind one minute, then like this the next?

"I think you're good for her," Brig says, giving me pause. "You're...the sun to her rain cloud. A rainbow," she says, trailing her fingers through the air in an arc. "She's been through some shit, just remember that, okay? Everyone deserves love."

"They do," I agree, relaxing.

Brig smiles and leans back on her elbows. "If you

love her, fuck 'em," she says, nodding to Natalie's retreating form.

Addison appears a few minutes later, plopping onto the sand next to me. "What did I miss?" she asks.

"The usual – Natalie trying to scare away your girl. Don't worry, Melody set her straight."

"She did what?" Addison asks, her shoulders slouching.

"Melody said you deserve better friends than Natalie," Brig said.

Addison looks down at the ground, her fingers trailing through the sand.

"C'mon, let's play frisbee," Brig says, pulling us to our feet to teach me another game. I am terrible at it, but Addison and I laugh and dive.

It's an almost perfect day.

15

ADDISON

Melody's forehead presses against the passenger window, her breath fogging it as she sleeps. She took a short nap on the beach, but otherwise, she'd kept up with my friends.

She said you deserve better friends.

Maybe I do, but they're what I have. A group of sad, lonely creatures drawn together. When shit hits the fan, I can count on at least one of them. Never the same one, and never all at the same time. That's the strength of a group like that – numbers.

Melody, with her loving family and open heart, would never understand. Someone like Stefan or Samira would chew her heart to pieces. As friends, they'd be fine, as long as she didn't expect too much from them. If she'd met *them* under that pier and not me...well.

We pull up to the house, and I reach over to touch her shoulder, rousing her.

"Hey, we're home," I say.

She yawns and stretches, rubbing the sleep out of her eyes. Her post-nap smile is lazy, and I want to kiss it. So, I do. I lean over the seat and our lips meet, stoking a fire low in my belly.

"Let's go inside," I say.

Once through the door, Melody wraps her arms around me, pulling me close to her. Her lips meet mine again – slow, sensual, her tongue darting out to flick against my own. I groan into her mouth, and I feel her smile.

"To bed?" I say.

"To bed," she agrees.

But we don't untangle from each other. Her fingers trail along the bottom of my shirt, sliding under to tease the skin there. She traces a line from my lower back to my abdomen, pushing upward until she's running her fingers under my bikini top. Her fingers are under the loose material quickly, circling a nipple. She ducks her head to lick along my other nipple, drawing it to attention.

"Mmm," she murmurs into my skin. "You taste like the beach."

"I can shower real quick..." I start, but Melody is insistent, pressing me hard against the wall.

"I want to lick it off your skin." The idea sends a

bolt of heat through my body, joining with the sensation of her lips on my nipples. We need to move this to my room before Emilio or one of my other roommates comes out and sees me having sex in the living room.

"C'mon," I say, taking her hand and leading her to my room, shutting the door behind us with my foot. Her mouth is on mine immediately, pressing me against the door. She's still smaller than me, but the last week of raw fish has softened her bony edges. I want her to consume me, to cover every inch of me with herself.

She pulls my shirt over my head and tosses it to the side, my bikini top following closely behind. She steps back, her gaze roving my half-naked body with unrestrained hunger. I can see now why she considers herself part animal. She is all but feral as she reaches for me, tossing me onto the bed. I squirm out of my shorts and bottoms, spreading myself for her.

Her gaze snaps to my pussy and she moves toward it, then hesitates. Her eyes flick to mine as she crawls over my body, lowering her head to my neck. She gives it a long, languid lick from my shoulder to my jawline, moaning at the taste.

She proceeds to lick and taste a slow, agonizing journey down my body. The farther she goes the more insistent she becomes, patience abandoned as she moves closer and closer to my aching core. By the time she's made it to my abdomen, I can't sit still, my hips bucking toward her in hopes of speeding her up.

"Please," I beg.

"Please what?" she asks from my hip bone, her teeth dragging delightfully across the sensitive skin there. When I jump ,she places her hands on my hips, holding me down.

"Please," I say again, unable to bring myself to say the words. Dirty talk has never been my forte, probably because I've spent my life never voicing what I truly want. I was a disruptive child, I'm a disruptive adult, and it's best to keep things to myself. Expressing needs, wants – that was the fastest way to get reprimanded, for people to leave me.

"Please what?" she repeats, her mouth lifting from my skin. All she needs to do is move a few inches south and she'd be there. I'm so wet it slides between my cheeks and puddles on the bed below. I've never been teased before – never *allowed* myself to be teased before.

"Can you please..." I squirm, this time with discomfort. "Can you...I want you to...Jesus, fuck, Melody don't look at me like that. I want your mouth on me, I want to cum. Please..." It's the right thing to say. Her mouth lowers to my aching pussy and she sucks my lips into her mouth, her teeth nudging at the hood over my sensitive clit as she does so. My head falls back, and my hips rise to her face.

She feasts like she's starved.

Her tongue moves from my clit to my opening, alternating between sucking on me and slipping her tongue deep inside me. Her fingers curl against my ass cheeks, pulling me close to her mouth, keeping with my incessant bucks and thrusts. My first orgasm is quick, spurred by the long teasing of her tongue on my hot skin.

She doesn't back off – her lips stay where they are. This time, though, she adds a finger, then two, pumping me toward another orgasm. She curls her fingers just as I'd done to her, and the second orgasm hits shortly after the first dies down.

Still, she doesn't move. She backs off my clit a little now, placing tender kisses along the side of the sensitive bud as I flinch and jump at her motions. She moves to kiss along my inner thigh, teeth gently scraping the skin there. A third finger joins her other two inside me, pumping slowly as I come down from the second orgasm.

"You taste like the ocean," she breathes against my thigh. "You taste like home," she says, quieter – so quiet I almost don't hear it. Before I can speak, her mouth is on my clit again, attacking it with renewed fervor. Her fingers increase their pace, angling to reach deep inside of me.

You taste like home. You taste like home.

No one has ever said something like that to me. No

man or woman has ever pulled me close, told me they cared, *showed* me they cared. Melody moves her lips as though she can prove it through orgasm alone. My third one hits like a freight train, and I'm dragged under by the explosion of sensation across my core. I cry out, not caring how loud I'm being, my fingers curling in Melody's hair to hold her there. She doesn't shy away but she does slow as she eases me through the third, powerful orgasm. Her lips and fingers slow until I'm little more than a shaking, trembling mess on the bed.

She slides up my body, licking my release from her fingers before pulling me tightly against her. I press my head against her chest, listening to her heart as it thunders beneath her ribs. Her fingers draw long, slow patterns along my shoulders and back. We lay like this until my body stops tremoring and I feel more like a human and less like a wet blanket.

"I'm starving," Melody says, rolling out of bed. I mourn the loss of her body, still floating on the high from the multiple orgasms.

"There's still food in the cooler," I tell her. "It's in my trunk."

She nods and adjusts her clothes, closing the bedroom door quietly behind her.

What a day.

Taking her to meet my friends was a gamble, but I needed to know. I needed to know if she would run away at the slightest friction, or if she'd stay close. Maybe I didn't need to keep the skin for a few weeks? Maybe today was the perfect test, the perfect proof? But I think again of what she said in those waves, how she talked about returning home once she got it.

Thinking of her skin sitting in the trunk of my car turns my stomach. I roll onto my side, pulling my arms tight around my middle. I'll tell her – I will. I'll just have to think of a way that doesn't make it seem like I've had it for a full 24 hours and never mentioned it. I just need assurance that she'll stay if I give it back to her, that she'll check in with her family and come back to me in the end.

It hurts, but that's life...right? I have too many questions I need answered before I give her back her skin.

If she left, I'd....

Her skin.

In the trunk of my car.

I sit upright, sucking in a breath. I fumble with the light, nearly knocking the lamp over in the process. How the fuck did Melody not trip over all this shit on her way out? I meant to clean up when I got home from work the other day, fuck. I stumble over the piles of clothes, grabbing anything I can find to cover up. Fuck, I'll wear the bed sheet if it means I can get to her first.

I'm too late.

The street lights are on now that the sun is down,

illuminating her frozen figure. Her hand is outstretched, her fingers paused mid-air.

"Melody, wait!" I call.

When she turns her face toward me, it's covered in tears.

"Melody, just wait..." I say, stepping out of the house and into the yard. Her head jerks back to the trunk, her fingers curling around the skin. It's large and unwieldy, but she pulls it against her body easily, holding it close. She closes her eyes and presses her nose into it, breathing deeply.

I fucked up.

Seeing her like this, the tears, the way she clutches the skin like it's a lifeline...

My heart fractures into a million pieces.

She holds the skin against her body, her fingers splaying over it, caressing it like an old friend. And I hid it from her, kept it in my *trunk*. My dirty, nasty trunk. I should have given it to her right away. I should have hidden it somewhere better, somewhere cleaner.

Anything to erase the hurt on her face as she turns to me again.

Betrayal. Heartbreak.

Because of me.

I step toward her. She steps away.

No. I have to fix this.

"You found it," I say, babbling. "I wasn't sure, I meant to show you, but I forgot. I kinda found it on accident, you know. I wasn't even sure it was yours, didn't want to get your hopes up..."

"How long?" she asks, her voice muffled by the skin. It's against her face now, her eyelids flutter as she breathes it in.

"Not long, just like..." I trail off, averting my gaze to the sky. Movement on the street makes my gaze snap back to her, to see Melody walking away from me. She stomps, a determined clack of her sandals against the sidewalk. If I go back inside to grab my shoes I'll lose her – I have to follow.

"Melody!" I say, picking up my pace. She moves faster, not once turning back to look at me. "So, it is your skin – great! I'm so glad! I just...I didn't want to give you the wrong thing. I didn't..." I trail off, spiraling. What can I say? What lie can I concoct to make myself not the villain in this?

We move through the few blocks to the ocean, me desperately trying to keep up with Melody as we enter the crowded streets. It's Saturday night and the boardwalk is alive with motion and color. I slow to avoid stepping on glass with my bare feet, and when I look up she's gone.

"Melody!" I cry over the buzz of the crowd. Some people turn to stare, but most ignore me as I elbow through them.

Where the fuck did she go?

Blonde hair catches my attention as she clears the

concrete barrier and down onto the dark beach below. I hop after her, slipping and sliding down the sand as I try to gain on her.

The beach sits vacant under the boardwalk. The only lighting comes from the boardwalk and the moon as it rises over the waters on the horizon. It's full, heavy, casting bright yellow light on the world below. I'm almost to her now – she paused at the edge of the water to start to put the skin on.

How? I haven't the faintest idea, I'd looked it over a few times and it made no logical sense how she could wear it – much less breathe in it.

It's not her skin, it's some weird thing you paid too much money for, I reason. Once she tries to put it on she'll realize, and she'll come back to me. She won't leave, she'll stay and we'll laugh about it. Remember when you found that old thing in my trunk and thought it was your skin? Hahaha!

The shadows cast by the boardwalk overhead make it hard to understand what I see. Melody stands knee-deep in the water, her clothing discarded on the beach behind her. Water licks at the edges of her sundress, and one sandal catches in the tide and floats to her. Her bare back is exposed to me, her muscles shifting as she slips her arms into the skin.

She's going into the water.

"Melody, wait! The tide...it's too strong right here! You can't!" I trip in the sand, crawling my way to my feet. I only dare go as deep as my ankles, I've seen the posters about the hidden rip tides. They will tear even the strongest swimmer away from the shore, sometimes drag them underwater in the process.

Melody takes one last glance over her shoulder at me. Her wide, soulful eyes are tear-filled, streaking down her pale face. She looks like the woman I found under this exact boardwalk just a week prior, lost and confused. This time she isn't just crying because of her skin...she is crying because of *me*.

I did this. I'm the reason she wades into the dangerous waters to her demise, slipping the rest of the way into that death trap of a wet suit.

"No!" I cry, my voice a broken croak as I lunge for her. She turns away from me and dives into the water, her entire body disappearing into the waves.

"Help! Lifeguard...someone!" I scream at the empty beach. I turn back to the waves, afraid to see her flailing body as she drowns.

Instead, two wide eyes stare back at me – the eyes of a seal. Its head bobs above the surface of the waves, catching the light from the boardwalk and stars above. It watches me for a long moment before turning to swim back into the ocean.

I'd recognize those eyes anywhere. I stared into them all week, wanting to memorize every color in the iris, every orgasm, every emotion. It's Melody – and I've lost her.

16

MELODY

The ocean greets me like an old friend.

My skin – my skin! Dirty, mistreated by whatever human had it in their possession.

Addison. Addison had it.

Selkies cannot cry in their seal form. Whatever noise I make is a product of my human side, sobs swallowed by the riptide that carries me away from that boardwalk. I need the bright colors of the humans as far away from me as possible. I can't stand to look at them; every winking light reminds me of Addison.

Every kick of my tail is another foot, another mile away from what hurt me, even after it promised it wouldn't. She was just like the humans of the past, the ones my ancestors warned me about. All her kind gestures were not for me – they were for her. To keep me there with her, to make me stay against my will.

But it wasn't against my will, not really. If she'd asked, I would have stayed. I would have spent my days in the ocean and returned at night, knowing I had a safe place for my skin.

But she never asked.

She just took.

It didn't matter when she'd found the skin, or even if she had it the whole time. It was all the same.

She lied.

My vision blurs as I swim harder, faster – I must get home. I've never been gone this long; my family will know. I'm sure if I went to their normal beachside resting spots I would have seen them, looking for me, speaking to other selkie pods to see if I'd wandered off.

When I return, they surround me with their bubble of love. We brush on each other, faces pressed against each other, whiskers tickling. They tell me how much they missed me, that they're glad that I'm safe, that I've always had a home with them.

Forever, no matter what.

I tell them of the mistake I made – of the human I trusted.

We warned you, say the elders.

Love is dangerous, say the others.

Love? Did I love Addison?

I suppose I loved her, maybe. Loved what I thought she was.

I loved her mind, the way it could jump from one

topic to the next and back within the same breath. I loved the way she pulled me close at night. I loved that she made me fish, even though she hated the smell. I loved that she never questioned me when I told her what I needed, even when others stared. She would simply nod and make it happen.

But those things – they were lies. I was something she wanted to own, something that she had to trap on land. If it were real, if she were true with her intentions, she wouldn't need to hide my skin from me. She would know that if I got it back, I'd return to her.

That I'd always return to her.

My bed is lonely, and my heart is broken, but I am alive.

And free.

And alone.

17

ADDISON

Apparently, if you scream on the beach at night, the cops get called on you.

I have no idea what to say to them. *My girlfriend ran into the waves and turned into a seal.* Instead, I pretend to be drunk and the minute they turn, I run. Still barefoot, with Melody's abandoned dress and sandal clutched in my hands.

When I return home Emilio is pissed. I left the front door open, and I woke him from his early evening nap with all my screaming. He's understandably pissed, but what the hell am I supposed to say?

I pace my bedroom until I realize my feet are bleeding, which I tracked all over the discarded clothes on my bedroom floor. I shove the dirty clothes into a pile and deposit them in the bathtub, which I fill with cold water because I'm pretty sure that's how you remove blood.

Oh, shit, yeah – I'm bleeding.

I scrub my feet in the sink as best as I can, careful to extract the pebbles lodged in the skin. Do I have bandaids? Will bandaids on my feet work? They'll just fall off, and there's nothing grosser than a used bandaid on the ground. I gag at the thought of finding one under a pile of clothes or in the corner of the kitchen covered in hair.

I settle for a maxi-pad with socks over it. What's the difference between a bandaid and a pad, truly? It's more comfortable, though the heavy flow one makes squeaking noises as I walk. Whatever, no one will hear.

Jesus – the abandoned cups in this room.

I collect those next, loading up the dishwasher. It's already mostly full, so I can only put a few of them in… I'll fill the rest when –

Shit. There's still fish in my trunk, and I bet it smells.

It does. And my trunk was left open, which I didn't notice when I returned home. Thankfully there was nothing to steal, the cooler is probably older than I am. What the fuck do I do with the fish? Leave it out so Melody can smell her way back, like a cat that ran out the front door?

Shit – did Garbage run away? No, she's perched on

the couch, watching me knowingly. She ducks her head to try to look behind me.

"Sorry, bud – Melody's gone. Turns out she's a seal, and when she was reunited with her magical skin, she turned into it. Like...the opposite of the clock striking midnight and pumpkins." The cat says nothing, she just puffs up and trots away.

The fish – what do I do with it? The fridge will do for now. I put it in a Tupperware container because the smell is really strong. Hopefully, that will trap it in. The cooler can go in the backyard so I can rinse it out tomorrow.

Did I lock my car?

Yes – the trunk is closed, the car is locked.

Can I wear shoes over my pad-socks? What the fuck do I do tomorrow? I don't work, so I could just lay around here. Maybe in 36 hours when I return to work, I'll be able to wear normal shoes. There's no way I can fit the pad-sock combo into some business-appropriate shoes.

Back in my bedroom – oh, yeah, I was cleaning. I throw my clothes into my hamper then pause at the sight of Melody's sundress and one sandal. Her bathing suit is gone, it must have floated away too, lost to the water or sand. I sit on the floor and pull her dress into my lap, bringing it to my face to inhale.

I'm struck with the image of her holding her skin

against her, fingers splayed, tears running down her cheeks.

Your fault your fault your fault.

Fuck – the edge of the sundress is soaked from the ocean. I wipe my face, which is also wet. How did that happen? That makes no sense. Oh, Jesus, I'm crying. I'm sitting on my floor, holding a sundress in my lap, sobbing.

You only knew her one week. She just gave you attention, that's all. This is an attention thing, not a love thing.

Love. How could you love someone so fast? How could you love someone that you didn't even believe? She told me time and time again that her skin was important, that she needed it. I can't blame myself for not believing she was a fucking mythical creature, but I can blame myself for downplaying her needs. So what if her skin were metaphorical? It was important to her.

And I disregarded that. And then – when caught – I'd lied.

Tried to save face.

I collapse back onto my floor, staring up at the ceiling. The fucking fan is so dusty, how does it accumulate dust when it's always in motion? How does dust even land on it? I don't even think I have a stepladder high enough to reach, I'll have to get a chair and hope I don't die in the process.

Something digs into my back – it's the sandal. I turn it over in my hands. How fairy tale – one sandal, a generic size, worn only one day. But I know what Melody looks like – I'd know her eyes anywhere. The seal had her eyes, that's how I knew she didn't die and get reincarnated as a seal instantly, like in that book about the rabbit and scarlet fever.

It was her.

I'd know those eyes anywhere.

I'd know those eyes anywhere.

I could find her. I could...I could find her, and I could explain. If she came back to the boardwalk I'd known. Or maybe not the boardwalk, she'd be avoiding me. Where the fuck else do seals congregate?

I pull out my phone and start to search –

Seals in Southern California.

Selkies.

Selkie mythology.

Are selkies real?

Seal hangouts in San Diego.

Do seals hibernate?

Do seals migrate?

Damnit, I'm going to find her. I'll make it right.

DAY ONE – Sunday.

I start early, heading straight to the boardwalk. It's the closest, and the crowds don't pop off until late morning or early afternoon. The breeze is a little too crisp for morning beach-going, so it's mostly surfers. Except, the waves here aren't great this morning, so the beach is deserted. I follow the shore below the boardwalk, then I go out as far on the boardwalk as I can. No sign of seals.

This would be easier if I could enlist a friend – but how? "Hey, Brig – want to come look for a seal that looks like that woman you met for a few hours yesterday? No reason."

I'm alone on this.

I try again in the afternoon, trying to see any sign of sea life in the ocean. The sun is too bright and, combined with the waves, I have no idea what I'm looking at. Seaweed, pollution, who fucking knows?

By evening I've seen nothing, so I return home. I have to work tomorrow, so I'll have to wait until I'm off to search again. I have all the seal spots in San Diego saved (*Sally sells sea shells by the sea shore...fuck, that makes me think of Melody. Don't cry*) in my maps app to explore tomorrow.

Day Two – Monday.

I work all day, but the minute the clock strikes 5 pm I'm gone. La Jolla is a popular place for seals and sea lions. I had to research the difference – seals don't have ears, sea lions do. Which is wild, because Melody definitely has ears. I remember tracing my tongue along the edges of them.

La Jolla is huge and filled with a ton of people. And kids – holy fuck, why aren't they in school? It's a Monday, after all.

La Jolla has a ton of spots for seals and sea lions. I go to the cove first, because that's the easiest way to get close to them. I don't own binoculars, and I don't even know where I'd find them, so this is the only way I'll be able to recognize her.

It's a bust – there are a ton of people holding signs and screaming at anyone who goes onto the beach. I want to tell them I'm looking for one seal in particular, I'm not going to bother any of them, but the words die on my tongue as I look over the concrete wall. It's all sea lions, no seals. What a waste.

Day Three – Tuesday.

Back to La Jolla, this time to some place called kids beach or children's beach or little fucking screaming children beach. It's aptly named, and manmade, which is weird for California. I thought only billionaires were allowed to destroy the environment here?

Har har har.

The beach is full of kids running and screaming. A few seals are off to the side on the rocks, close enough to see but dangerous to try to get near. One eyes me up as I get as close as I dare, peering at all of their faces.

"Hey," I whisper-yell. "Hey – can you open your eyes? Like, the rest of you?"

They ignore me. The one closest to me narrows its eye – I swear to god – as if it can understand me. "Are you a selkie too? I'm looking for one – Melody."

The seal blinks. Maybe it doesn't understand what I'm saying, and it's just a typical seal, and I'm inter-rupting its nap time. Maybe it's a selkie and it's waiting for me to state my case. Can they talk in seal form? Unlikely, the skin didn't have a voice box.

"Do you know her? Melody – she's usually around the boardwalks. She was missing for a week, but she should be back to you guys by now. I need to talk to her. Can you find her? Do you know her?"

"HEY LADY!" a little kid yells from the sand. "DON'T BOTHER THE SEALS."

"I'M NOT," I shout back, though I guess I kind of am.

"SURE LOOKS LIKE IT," the kid yells back. The child is somewhere between the ages of 1 and 12, with curly reddish hair poking out from under a large bucket hat. It's wearing long sleeves and shorts, leaving only an inch of pale skin to peak through.

"Didn't your parents ever tell you to mind your own business?" I shoot back, edging away from the seals.

The kid smiles, triumphant at my retreat. "Didn't your parents ever tell you to leave wildlife wild?"

Fucking kid.

Day Four – Wednesday.

La Jolla again. This time I start with the glass beach area, one that is less likely to have people in it. No seals.

Back to the children's beach – no seals.

Ugh.

Back to the cove, where there are fewer people with signs. A few seals skirt the edges of the beach, so I tiptoe down and get as close to them as I can without being obvious. I sit in the sand and stare over the water, as though I was just a normal woman looking over the waves.

"Psst," I say to the nearest seal. It flinches and I curse, waiting for one of the sign people to yell. They don't notice, so I continue.

"I'm sorry – didn't mean to freak you out. Do you know a selkie named Melody? I need to talk to her." I chance a sideways glance, just in time to see the seal move away from me. Fuck, if I move now, it'll be obvious.

The moon is out by the time I make it back home, where I wander the boardwalk.

Nothing.

Day Five – Thursday.

I skip La Jolla because the thought of the crowds and struggling for a paid parking spot makes my skin crawl. Instead, I wander the boardwalk. I've invested in binoculars, but the sun is too bright, and I can't see shit. I even try the big ones on the boardwalk that make you pay a quarter. All I see is bright bright bright.

I sit under the boardwalk on the rocks until the noise of the people above subsides.

Day Six – Friday.

What's the point?

La Jolla – I'll brave the Friday crowds. I have to, after all. It's the only place I've seen a single fucking seal. I strike out everywhere except the cove, but the people with posters are there again. I try to sneak down to the beach, but a person stops me.

"Are you aware that it's breeding season for the sea lions?" he asks.

"Uh, what?" I reply. They have seasons? They're not like humans, where they can fuck year-round?

"It's breeding season," the man replies, as though talking to a child. "You'll get attacked if you get too close."

"Listen, buddy," I say, because I'm at the end of my fucking rope as it is. I'm generally a negative on the patience scale, and this week has been a *test*. Going to work every day, wandering the beach for my lost girlfriend by night...it's not how I envisioned my week.

"I don't plan to get anywhere near the fucking sea lions. I just want to go down to the beach, and sit near the seals," I continue, shouldering past him.

"You can see the seals from up here," he argues.

"Yeah, but I can't fucking talk to them from up here, now can I? They don't have fucking ears, so they can't hear me from all the way up here!" I shoot back. This surprises him enough to hesitate, which allows me to continue down into the cove. I give the sea lions plenty of space – which I would have done even not knowing it's their breeding season. They move fast, and I'm pretty sure I saw a viral video of a few of them absolutely body-checking tourists last year.

No thanks, I'm not in the mood to be shared across social media.

"Hey there," I say to the nearest seal, sure to keep my distance. There are a few other humans on the beach, mostly tourists snapping photos on their cameras, standing awkwardly in front of the sea lions.

The seals are forgotten, but I keep my voice down anyway.

"You happen to know a selkie? One named Melody? I don't know if you all communicate or what, but...I need to talk to her."

The seal watches me, its head tilted ever so slightly. It's the most encouraging thing I've had so far. I chance a slow, small step toward it. "Yeah, I'm Addison – I...I know Melody, I knew Melody. Anyway, I need to talk to her. Can you pass a message along? That I'd like to speak to her? At the boardwalk?"

The seal opens its mouth, and my eyes bug out of my head. Is this another selkie? Can it speak in its seal form? Holy shit it's happening! It's—!

The seal lets out the most terrifying noise I've ever heard before it charges at me. They're much slower on land than the sea lion, but I get the fucking point. I'm up the stairs and off the beach, nearly colliding with the man with the sign. He smirks at me and I...I don't know what comes over me, but the hurt and anger come to the surface. Not at him or the seal – they're just living their lives – but at *me*.

I'm the one that lied.

I'm the one that kept things from Melody.

I'm the one that doesn't deserve her at all.

Tears prick the backs of my eyes, and I turn to look down at the beach, over the concrete wall. "ALL I WANT TO DO IS APOLOGIZE," I scream down to the seals. The people on the beach turn to stare up at me, shading their eyes.

"I KNOW I FUCKED UP, I'M ALWAYS DOING THAT. I JUST WANT TO TELL HER SORRY, OKAY? THAT IT'S MY FAULT. BUT GO AHEAD, CHASE ME OFF THE BEACH YOU FUCKING SEAL. ENJOY YOUR BREEDING SEASON, YOU FUCKING DICK."

I run to my car before I get the cops called on me *again*.

18

MELODY

I shouldn't miss her, but I do.

The elders tell me stories of the humans that trapped them on land. Some are their own stories; most are passed down from selkie to selkie. Bedtime stories, and warnings about humans. If you must breed, if you must procreate, do so with your heart in a cage. Do not let them see it, don't let them touch it and don't – no matter what – fall in love.

Love. Is that what it was?

No – but it was something. It was the stars before the moon, it was the dawn before the day. It was a promise, a bud, something I could nurture into love.

I see now why they advised against it – Addison's feelings for me may not be real, but the pain in my chest is. The way I see things and think of her or want to hear what she thinks of it. I miss her quick mind, the way it can float from one topic to another as though they're all connected in an endless web.

I want to tell her about my day.

I want to laugh and sit on the boardwalk.

I miss the sun on my face, I miss those stupid glasses I had to wear to see during the day.

I miss her bed.

My sisters keep me company. "With time the ache will ease," says Penelope, her whiskers brushing mine.

"There'd be no ache if she listened to the warnings," says Drucella. She's older and bears a scar over her lower abdomen from a child she had while in human form. She says they took it from her, and she never saw it again. "We tell these stories because it's a reminder. Learn from our experiences, and just be glad yours was so short."

I should be glad that it was only a week, that I wasn't locked up, that I cared for my captor.

Captor? That can't be right. She never locked me inside…just took away my ability to leave.

"Melody, you've always been a dreamer. An optimist. I'm sorry this is what happened to bring you to your senses," Drucella says. Her fin against my side is supposed to be a comfort but it feels cold, harsh, the scrape of rocks underfoot.

Penelope watches her swim away and head-butts me. "There's nothing wrong with being a dreamer," she tells me. "But maybe…dream a little smaller?"

I swim, because I don't know what else to do. I make laps around my family, I eat with them, I listen to them talk.

"...screaming at us," I hear, the tail end of a conversation with my cousin, Kylee. Her voice is low as she speaks. "It's not the first time, I've seen her at all the beaches, looking for seals. She can be discreet, but this time she lost it." My cousin laughs, and the other selkies do too.

"I chased her off the beach, should teach her a lesson," she continues. "She should stay far away from our kind, lest she hurts another one of us."

"You did the right thing," Drucella says. "We should continue to ignore her, to scare her away if we must. She'll lose interest, humans always do. Then Melody can move on and heal."

"I hate seeing her like this," Kylee agrees. "She is so dull right now, I miss her bright light."

"It did her good," Drucella says. "It's what she needed to learn the truth and get her head out of the sand. Humans are not our friends, they're a means to an end."

"You scared her away?" I whisper. They all turn, and I can't stand the look in their eyes – pity. But also, something more, something unkind. It reminds me of Addison's friends, the ones who would say things about her when she wasn't there. Unkind and kind, equally doled out.

My family loves me, I know this, but...I am my own selkie.

"That's not your right," I say, my voice wavering. My fins tremble with the energy it takes to keep calm. I want to explode, I want to yell, I want to rage...but I'm unsure how. I've never done that before; I've never stood up for myself like this.

"Melody," Drucella says, as though she's speaking to a child. "It hurts, but growth always does."

I leave before I can hear another word.

19

ADDISON

I tip the bottle against my lips, swallowing the last bit of liquid from it. It's some sort of beer, something cheap and disgusting that I got at the corner store. It'll do the trick. Isn't that what Friday nights are for? Drinking?

I start at the bars like I used to, but everything about it makes me sick. I hate every outfit I picked out, I hate every man and woman I see. Every drink is too sweet, every person too close to me. The music is too loud, the air too hot.

I want to rip my skin off. I have to get out of the bar, so I run into the night, grab some beer, and crawl onto the rocks beneath the boardwalk.

A week – not even! I didn't even make it a full week of looking for her before I gave up. She deserves someone better, someone who would fight for her day in and day out until they found her. She deserves someone who won't give up after one, tiny little inconvenience.

I guess that isn't me. I guess I'm the woman who screams at seals on a beach.

I can't blame her – what do I even have to offer? What do I even bring to our relationship? Most of my friends suck and she doesn't like them. I have a joke of a job that I'm overqualified for. I live with roommates despite flirting with thirty. My car is on its last leg like...four legs ago. I can't keep a coherent stream of thought. I'm not marriage material.

But, most importantly, I lied to her. I kept things from her. And when it mattered, when I should have, I didn't believe her.

I wouldn't come back to me either.

So – beer it is. I'll drown my sorrows in the shitty stuff, stumble back to my house, sleep the weekend away and try to regain some semblance of my life. Who am I kidding? I won't change. I'll go right back to the bars on the weekends, once the thought of touching anyone other than Melody doesn't make my skin crawl. I'll probably be fired from my job in the next few months.

Maybe it's good I fucked up so early? That way she didn't stick around long enough for the novelty to wear off. Her own little human, shiny and forbidden. Wait until my racing thoughts weren't cute anymore, or my chronic messiness began to border on biohazards. Then what? Back to the ocean for her, and back to the bars and meaningless connections for me.

I resist the urge to throw the glass bottle onto the rocks and watch it shatter. The thought of Melody or her seal selkie family getting the bits of glass in their fins makes me want to vomit.

Instead, I stand and pace, my toes digging into the wet sand. The salt from the ocean stings on my scabbed feet but I deserve it.

"You deserve it," I say aloud. "It's all your fault. All my fault...whatever." I cn't even monologue right. Soliloquy? Whatever, English is a stupid subject.

"*It's okay,*" the ocean whispers. It sounds like her, bright and optimistic. Now my racing thoughts are conjuring up voices to argue back. Not just any voice – *her* voice. Another way to punish myself, how awesome.

"It's really not," I bite out, laughing and shaking my head. "Listen, ocean – if you knew how I fucked up, you wouldn't say that. You'd leave me too."

I plop into the sand, not caring that my dress is now soaked. I'll look like I pissed myself, but whatever. I tilt my head back to gaze up at the boardwalk above, at the people milling overhead. "You know, nothing is ever my fault. At least, that's what I tell myself. Even when I knew I played a big part in my own downfall, I always found someone else to blame. My mom, my upbringing, my ... whatever this is," I say tapping my temple.

"But...it's also me, you know? It's always me, under the surface. Melody is..." I breathe out. "Kind. So kind. I used to think that was a bad attribute to have. If you're too nice, people will walk all over you. But she had her own strength, you know? Her kindness was a strength. I guess I thought that..." I shake my head and laugh. Earlier I screamed at seals, now I'm talking to the underside of the boardwalk.

"I guess I thought that gave me some ownership, maybe? No – that's not right, I never wanted to own Melody. She was afraid of that. Her family told her that's what humans do – they take, and they own. I guess we do, in a way. I took away her freedom, her choice. I was afraid she'd leave if given the option. I thought that by needing me, by relying on me, I could make her want me. No one's ever relied on me before, I've always been the unreliable one. I've always been the fuck up. But Melody didn't see me as that, she trusted me. It was...it was nice, being wanted, you know?

"But that doesn't make it right. I'm doing it again, I'm justifying it. I'm making myself the victim. Oh, feel bad for me – I'm such a screw up, take pity! No. It ends now. I need to realize that I am the problem. I am in control of my life and my life only. I have to accept that maybe…if she had a real reason, she would have stayed."

"*I had a reason*," the ocean says, but it's not the ocean.

It's her, bobbing in the surf, her blonde hair clinging to her face. She's naked, her bare shoulders just above the water. I want to run to her, to gather her in my arms and pull her close. I haven't earned the right, so I resist.

"Yes," I tell her, choking on a sob. "You had a reason – you needed your skin. And I found it, and I kept it from you because I knew once you had it, you'd leave."

"I would have stayed," she says. Each wave brings her closer, the water now just below her breasts.

"Don't," I say. "Don't do that, try to make me feel better."

"Are you calling me a liar?" she asks. The water is up to her waist now, that much closer.

"No," I say. "I'm calling you too good for me. I don't deserve you, Melody. You deserve someone who appreciates you, not someone who takes advantage of you. You deserve someone who puts you first, who doesn't lie to you for their own selfish needs."

"Maybe," she says. Now it's not the waves carrying her closer, but her feet. She kneels in front of me, a hand reaching out to cup my jaw. "Maybe I need to be more selfish. Why did you hide my skin from me?"

"Because I was scared," I admit on a whisper. "I was

scared that you didn't want the same thing. I was scared that you'd wake up one day and realize that the other humans in this world are so much better than me. When I found it, I froze, and I made the wrong decision. I was worried that you'd take it and you'd run home – away from me."

"I didn't run, I swam," she says. "And you should have given me the choice. You took it away. You can't do that again."

"Again?" I ask, because it holds so much promise. Again means a future with me in it.

"Yes," she says, her finger running along the side of my jaw. It's tender, but insistent. "We are imperfect beings, humans and selkies. You made a mistake."

"It was a royal fuck up," I argue.

"If you're trying to convince me to give you a second chance, you're doing a poor job. I have listened to you, now you listen to me – you are kind, Addison. Your mind wants you to jump to the worst conclusion first, but that is never the case with me. With me you can look at the bright side first, you can look at the possibilities and promises, not the dangers. You've shown me who you are inside, and it is different than who you say you are. You argue that – what – you are messy? You live with roommates? You don't like your job? These are not who you are, they are just your circumstances," she says.

She's closer now, her lips inches from mine. I want

to kiss her; I want to pull her to me and fall back into the sand with her. But it's not just about what I want – it's about her too.

"It's more than that," I whisper. "Was it kind of me to lie to you? I knew you'd leave if you found your skin, I should have realized it'd be my own fault. I don't take this second chance lightly; I want to spend every day proving that I've earned it."

"Promise?" she asks. Her lips skirt mine, then trace my jaw.

"Yes," I suck in a breath, and her lips are on mine.

The kiss is slow, measured, a reintroduction of our mouths. She prods gently with her tongue, then offers a little teeth. The sweet and the savory, the soft and the hard. I pull her close to me, wanting to never let her go.

"I don't forgive you, not yet. But I know how you can start earning me back."

20

———

MELODY

The boardwalk lights overhead illuminate the streaks of tears on Addison's face. I kiss the right streak, then the left. I missed the taste of her skin, I missed her body next to mine. She pulls me close and buries her face in my shoulder, her shoulders shaking as she cries.

"I'm sorry," she whispers.

I hold her at arm's length, resisting the urge to kiss her tears all over again until they dry on her skin. "I know," I tell her, tracing my fingers along her jaw. There is no triumph in this, only acceptance.

Our kiss is tender. She is slow, soft against my lips, even as her body shakes. I gather her close once more, pressing my wet skin against her clothed body. It's too much of a barrier, I want to pull it off and have nothing between us. No words, no worries, just skin on skin, heart to heart. She sighs into my mouth and her kiss deepens. I open my mouth to her, letting her tongue swipe mine. I suck on it, pulling back to catch her lip between my teeth. Her sigh becomes a groan, her fingers tightening on my arms.

"You said I can earn your forgiveness," she breathes. Her eyelids flutter as she watches me this close, gaze darting from my mouth to my eyes.

I nod, trying to stop the grin that tugs at the corners of my mouth. She will not be easily forgiven – it will take time to patch up the trust she shattered. That does not mean she cannot bribe me.

She leans into me, forcing me onto my back in the sand. The waves crash over my toes, and I curl them, able to be in the ocean and on land at the same time. Addison rests between my thighs, her gaze raking over my naked body. There's a wanting there, a hunger – like she never thought she'd see me again. I suppose I didn't know either.

Her fingers trail along my calves, kneading into the muscle there. A week on land, a week swimming – my muscles are unaccustomed to these changes. I tilt my head back into the sand and groan as she works her way from one calf to the other, digging into the tense muscle. She moves upwards when satisfied, rubbing the muscles along the sides of my thigh, then the meat of them. She's unhurried, her pace steady as she moves upward, closer and closer to my waiting sex.

I've missed these touches. My own hand is nothing compared to this. At night I tried to get myself off, only to find the ache of my heart was too great to cum. I don't want to wait anymore, and I wiggle my body toward her face.

I groan as she skips my waiting pussy and moves to my hips, her fingers digging into the muscles there. I catch her devilish grin before she can suppress it.

"Let me spoil you," she says softly.

I open my mouth to protest but she silences me with pressure on my hips, encouraging me to roll over onto my belly in the sand. I do as I'm told and she moves up my body, her legs straddling my hips. Her fingers return, this time to my back. She starts at my neck, rolling and squeezing the tired muscles there. It is so hard to keep a human head upright. I close my eyes and decide to enjoy the slow torture of her hands, sinking into the sand below.

She slides down my body as her hands get to my hips, then her fingers press into the soft swell of my ass cheeks. I hold still, resisting the urge to look over my shoulder and see what she does. She spreads my cheeks then pushes them together and upward, exposing my pussy from behind. Her hands travel downwards to the back of my thighs then my knees, pushing them forward. My face is still pressed to the sand, my ass now up in the air, my chest pressed into my thighs.

She slides a finger from just below my asshole to my pussy, dragging my wetness with her. Her finger continues, pushing forward through my folds until it's on my clit. She swirls it a few times, using her other hand to push two fingers inside me. I try to spread my legs, but she pushes them back together, her fingers stilling inside me. With my legs like this, I'm tighter over her fingers and she can angle them deeper into me. I push back against her fingers, trying to drive her deeper and harder into me.

She doesn't make me beg, doesn't make me wait – her fingers pick up speed, and she angles them deeper into me. Each thrust pushes my face against the sand, but I love the friction. Her other hand works my clit, slipping and sliding it around as my wetness coats her fingers and slips downward.

Her fingers curl, hitting a spot inside me and I cry out, letting the sand muffle my voice. She does it again, and again, increasing her speed. She adds a third finger and I'm so full I could explode. My orgasm isn't far away, it's skirting along my lower abdomen. She removes her fingers from my pussy, and my groan becomes a cry of anger at the emptiness. She shifts and the fingers return, alternating between deep thrusts and sliding over my clit.

She smears my wetness across my asshole, and I freeze, my breath caught in my throat. She stops what

she's doing, her words frantic. "Is this okay? I'm sorry –
I thought…"

"Yes," I say, pushing back against her. I want to feel
it, I want to know. This human body has so many
different sensations, so many different ways to wring
out pleasure. I want to know how this feels, if I like it or
not. And I want Addison to be the one to test it.

"You're sure?" she asks. Her fingers press against
the hole again, probing. I nod and she goes back to
sliding her fingers into my pussy, rocking her hand
along my clit. The pressure against my asshole is gentle
but insistent until it pops through the barrier. It's just
one finger, and just the tip of it, but the sensation is
unlike anything I've felt before.

My orgasm hits, and I clamp down on both her
fingers, pushing myself back into her hand. Her finger
in my ass slides in deeper and I peak higher. Her
fingers in my pussy slow to focus on my clit, light insistent touches until my orgasm backs off.

But she's not done with me. The finger in my ass
probes deeper, gently sliding in and out, adventuring a
little further each time. She alternates it with the
fingers in my pussy, tilting them upward as if they
could rub and meet. The friction of the two drives me
wild, and I have to swallow a cry as I feel another
orgasm building. She must feel it too, for she slows her
movements in both my ass and pussy, her touches
barely there until the orgasm fades.

Once I've stilled, her fingers move again with renewed fervor, fucking me and sliding over my clit. Before long I'm panting in the sand, pushing up on my elbows for more traction to push against her. I'm fucking myself on her, driving myself to an orgasm that barrels toward me like a ship through waves.

But she slows again, stops before I can come, and I groan with frustration. When I look over my shoulder, I catch her devilish smile. She winks at me before increasing the speed again, this time not slowing as I get closer to orgasm. I'm tense, waiting for her to stop, waiting for the orgasm to fade again. It doesn't, and she adds another finger to my asshole.

I explode with a cry, thrusting my ass back into her as I chase my orgasm higher and higher. It rips from my abdomen and radiates through my pulsing pussy and my now sensitive clit. Addison keeps pace with me, slowing only when my body starts to shake. I collapse onto my chest in the sand, unable to hold myself upright anymore.

Her fingers slide from me, and she gathers me in her arms. The tide has moved upward, now licking along my calves. Overhead, the stars wink down at me as the lights from the boardwalk turn off. I roll over to face Addison once I've recovered, kissing her jaw softly.

"Well?" she says, and I blink at her without understanding. "Am I a little closer to forgiveness?" I grin, burrowing my head in her chest.

"You've got a ways to go but...this was a good first step."

It is better this way – going between the selkie world and the human one.

Addison works during the week, so I return to the ocean to be with my family. None of them apologize, but none of them reprimand me either. They think I'm going to 'learn my lesson,' but I want to teach them one myself.

Life will hurt you. Sometimes it's a lover that hurts you, sometimes it's an enemy. It's more than the hurt, though. It's how they try to fix that hurt, how they try not to do it again. It's what they *show* you, not what they tell you.

Addison wants to make it right, and she knows it's more than in the bedroom.

It's a safe place to put my skin, with a lock and a key only I have access to. She even throws it on the ground a few times to show how sturdy the lock is, that she cannot break it and keep me captive.

It's the way she offers to meet my family, though the logistics are hard at first. They don't prefer to wear clothes on land, but they agree once they realize they're going to be fed. Dinners are once a month, and they leave with full bellies. By the third month, they still grumble, but it's between smiles.

I do my part, too. Even though she hurt me, it doesn't mean I can hold it over her forever. We are partners, she is the other half of my heart, so I must make her happy too. I learn to cook her human food, I clean from time to time, and – most importantly – I listen. The way her face lights up when I remember a coworker's name without prompting means more to me than gifts or pretty words.

The most important, I think, is that I am always myself. Even in my human form, I am always me, and I demand the same of Addison. She cannot hide her thoughts from me, I want to know them all. I want to trace the map of her mind with her, following her leaps and bounds around topics. She knows so much about this strange world she lives in – I want to know it too.

So I tell my family these things – that love is not linear. Love is not perfect, it's not without mistakes... but is it always with care. It is with acceptance and understanding.

So I will love Addison, and Addison will love me until we are nothing more than coral in the reef.

ABOUT THE AUTHOR

I often get asked, "Katryna, how did you come up with the idea for the Cryptids of America series?" The answer is simple; I was window shopping in Estes Park when I saw the plethora of Sasquatch merchandise, and I wondered would he would be DTF?

That's how I come up with all my ideas; I see something and think, "Man, what a wild story THAT would be." Then I look it up and see there isn't a story like that, get bummed... then fire up the old Mac and get to typing.

The Cryptids of America is written as a series of shorts that can be read in any order, the only purpose is to make your toes curl and your mother blush. I exclusively write stories with action in them; no fade to black here, but the focus of the stories varies. Other stories I write aren't the same - some are longer forms where the smut is just an added bonus.

To keep up with the latest releases, special editions, and bonus chapters, my website and newsletter are fantastic resources at <u>cm-deer.com/kll.</u>

Mitch and Tatiana's love was all dried up.

They moved to the Pine Barrens with one goal: capture evidence of the Jersey Devil. The evidence they received from an anonymous listener of their podcast - CryptidCore99 - was all they had to go on when they packed up their life and moved to the woods. A year later they had nothing to show for it except a crumbling relationship. With just a week left before their lease is up and they part ways, things are looking dire.

At least, until Tatiana runs into the Jersey Devil on a run.

Sexual tension runs high when The Jersey Devil finds

sketches of himself in interesting positions with humans in Mitch's backpack. Is this encounter exactly what this couple needed to reignite their spark? Or is this the final straw that breaks them apart?

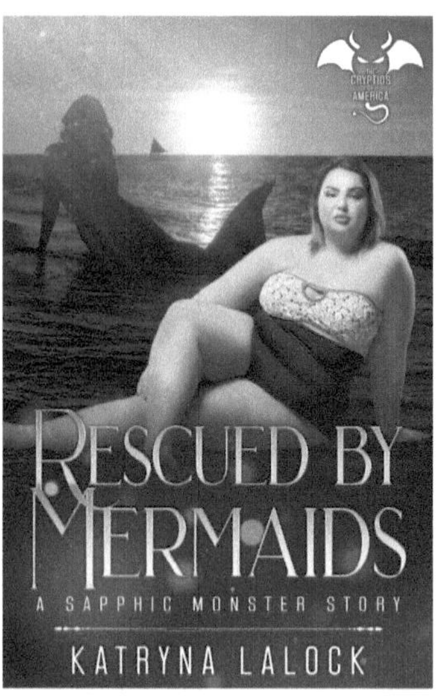

Hannah is lost on the ocean all because of a stupid work bet. If she hadn't let her stupid male coworkers upset her so much she wouldn't be in this position. It's day two lost off the shores of Florida and it looks like she's not going to survive this. She sings to pass the time, drawing the attention of a beautiful mermaid who rescues her and nurses her to health. Gabriella is beautiful and genuinely cares for Hannah. It doesn't take long for Hannah to fall in love with the dark haired beauty and her talented tongue.

Does Hannah even want to go back to the shore?

There were two creatures in this forest - one a god, one a monster. I was hunting the monster.

The forest god we worshiped for years may have given up on us, but I have not. After Greta was killed I vowed to stop the beast myself. I wasn't alone in the forest that night - our forest god watched. And once the beast was gone, I was the only creature they wanted.

Newly single Carmen is not having a good time. Her ex Elliott cheated on her and left her heartbroken and crying. Thankfully her best friend, Devan, had just the suggestion - a solo hiking/camping trip in the remote forest of the Rocky Mountain National Park. Being a seasoned hiker and camper Carmen is all too excited to spend a week off the grid in one of her favorite national parks.

The site is perfect. It has a clearing along the river that allows for afternoon swims, the perfect trees for her hammock and countless small trails to explore. Still, she can't shake the feeling she's not completely alone. This fact becomes abundantly apparent when a family of bears visit her. Carmen would be dead if it weren't for the large man covered in fur named Sam, who saved her before disappearing into the bush.

Who is Sam? WHAT is Sam? Why did Devan give her directions to this particular campsite, and why did she wink when she did? It turns out this particular clearing belongs to Sam the Sasquatch and he's known for helping people get over exes...by getting under someone else.

Eagle's Nest sinkhole in Florida is known as the Mount Everest for cave divers. Nate is no stranger to caves or danger - he's spent most of his life angry at the world and making bad choices. Eagle's Nest represents all of the obstacles he's overcome in his life and nothing can ruin this dive...except an inexperienced tag along who leaves Nate alone in the dark underwater caves. When a half woman, half octopus named Kali saves his life he wonders if he actually died or is suffering from hallucinations.

He also can't help wonder what her tentacles would feel like on his body.

SASQUATCH'S SEDUCTION

A MF MONSTERLOVER EROTICA

1
____

"The best way to get over someone is to get under someone else."

It's what Devan had said to Carmen just two days before, reaching across the table to give her friend's arm a sympathetic squeeze. Devan never liked Elliott; she thought he was pretentious, rude, and – to be honest – not handsome enough for Carmen.

Friends were always that way, weren't they? Assuming you were the sun and the men you associated with were dusty, old moths drawn to something too bright for them to handle. Carmen had tried not to cry at the time; she *hated* crying in public. She held back tears as she nursed her third mimosa during the bottomless brunch. It was an emergency girls' meeting after Elliott cheated on Carmen and blamed it on her.

On the drive home, Carmen had thought over

Devan's words as tears streamed down her face, obscuring her vision. Hastily, she'd wiped them away on her shoulder, both hands tightening on the steering wheel. The brunch had been much needed, but it hadn't filled the giant hole in her heart. After brunch, Devan had caught Carmen's arm before they parted ways.

"Here," she'd said, pressing a piece of paper into Carmen's hand. "This will get you what you need."

Carmen had opened the paper, reading the instructions as if in a daze. "A campsite?" she'd asked, her brow furrowed.

Devan had smiled, her eyes far away as she nodded. "Yes, a campsite. A remote one in Rocky Mountain National Park. It's not *strictly* a campsite." She'd given her friend a conspiratorial wink, her eyes twinkling with mischief.

Carmen nodded mutely and shoved the paper into her pocket.

A few days later, as she emptied her pockets looking for her mail key, she remembered the paper. She flattened the crumpled paper – her fingers tracing the instructions.

She needed to get away; everything in her apartment reminded her of *Elliott*. Netflix's latest binge-worthy dating show only reminded her of nights curled on the couch, gasping at the dysfunctional couples. He'd sounded so reasonable against that backdrop. All that talk he'd spewed: "Man, if they just went to THERAPY! The cornerstone of any relationship is trust. Honestly, it's like no one communicates anymore."

As if he wasn't lying and cheating at the same time.

Even the stupid decorative pillows she placed on her bed reminded her of him! He'd toss them on the floor and shake his head. "Who are you decorating for?" he'd say before nestling under the covers. No matter how many times she told him to keep them off the floor they ended up there, night after night. Tightening her fist over the paper at the memory that surfaced in her mind, she made her choice.

Carmen packed her overnight bag for a camping trip. It wasn't her first; that's how she'd met Devan and the rest of her friends. She hadn't known a soul when she moved to Fort Collins, Colorado. Through hiking, she'd run into a group of like-minded people who loved the outdoors as much as she did. She'd spent the last three summers working on her Chaka tan line and learning the finer points of instant coffee and campsite meals.

It'd been too long since Carmen solo camped. The last few weeks of constant brunches, time with friends, quick hikes, and long phone calls were great to take her mind off Elliott. She needed to really recharge, to be alone with her thoughts instead of burying.

Tears welled in her eyes as she turned into Estes

Park, heading toward Rocky Mountain National Park. She swiped them away, angry at herself for still being upset weeks after the breakup. In a split decision, she pulled into the parking lot to grab a slice of pie from You Need Pie! It was her favorite place to eat after a long day of hiking in the park. This time she used it as fuel before getting started, settling on a ginger mango slice before entering the park at last.

Devan's instructions were detailed and involved a little bit of off-roading. "Don't worry," the paper said. "It's not on a map. Not because it's illegal, but because it's special." They were the strict leave no trace types; there's no way Devan would have her off-roading through a protected area. Carmen nearly missed the turnoff, reveling at the sound of the tires of her Jeep on a dirt road. She continued to bump along the road, stopping here and there to take pictures on her phone of the snow-capped mountains. It always amazed her that the air could be so cold even in the summer, the mountains still covered with snow. She was from northern Mexico, where summer seemed never to end. This... this was a unique and exotic beauty, like none she'd ever seen before.

The dirt road tapered to a stop at a beautiful campsite. A fire circle sat in the middle of the small clearing, spectacularly shaded by a large tree. A tributary gurgled just a few feet from the clearing. Small bushes edged the clearing, their branches heavy with ripe berries. It was perfect, and for the first time in weeks, Carmen's heart soared. She turned her Jeep around so the trunk opened to the clearing and unloaded her tent and supplies.

Once her Jeep was emptied, Carmen reclined in the folding chair she brought, listening to the music of nature – the bubbling tributary, the sound of birds chirping, the wind delicately stroking the tree overhead. Despite the heavenly silence, Carmen couldn't help but shake the feeling of eyes on her, watching her every movement.